THE
HITCH
knots that bind

THE
HITCH

knots that bind

DonnaLee
OVERLY

Giro di Mondo

The Hitch Copyright © 2019 by DonnaLee Overly

For permission, please write to Giro di Mondo Publishing, a division of the Ottima Group, 1417 Sadler Rod, Suite 332, Amelia Island, FL 32034, or email info@girodimondo.com.

Printed in the United States of America.
First Edition, June 2019
10 9 8 7 6 4 3 1 0

Cover and Interior design by Roseanna White Designs
The Hitch Knot artwork by DonnaLee Overly

Library of Congress Control Number: 2019935210

ISBN Trade Paperback- 13: 978-0-9966687-7-4
 E-BOOK: 13: 978-0-9966687-9-8

www.girodimondo.com

This book is dedicated to all who have suffered from depression and addiction and also to those who care and love them.

"Every artist dips his brush in his own soul, and paints his own nature into his pictures."
– Henry Ward Beecher (June 24, 1813 – March 8, 1887)

PART 1

CHAPTER  1

Gabby watches her baby wave his small arms back and forth and her lips curve upward. She offers him her forefinger and he reaches for it and grasps tightly. His strong grip surprises her. As she looks down at his face, his eyes remind her of her daddy's. Already this little one has captured her heart with his bright eyes and sweet coos.

"I love you, my son." The kiss from her lips reveals the softness of his cheek, and his gentle breath is intoxicating. She closes her eyes in amazement, and she marvels at the joy of motherhood.

"Gabby, Gabby..." A familiar voice calls but it is a faint echo. "I love you, Gabby. Please, don't leave me. You promised."

Yes, it is Brett's voice. She is excited to introduce him to little Jacob, the name they picked to honor Brett's father. Her smile widens as thoughts of their future dance in her head. They'll be happy. She is certain. A new trinity knot is created; it is her trinity knot that symbolizes her new family—Brett, Gabby, and Jacob. They are the three loops of the knot held together by their circle of love.

Suddenly aware that her arms are empty, Gabby yells, "Jacob, Jacob, where are you?" Her heart is racing and her breathing quickens. She struggles to move but her limbs are heavy and numb. Why can't she move? Why can't she open her eyes? Where is Jacob? All goes black.

During the wee hours of this night, twenty-nine-year-old Gabby King lies unconscious in the critical care unit after a placental abruption that sadly took her son's life, and her fiancé anxiously keeps vigil by her bedside.

Earlier that evening

"Buckle in, Mr. Matthews," the medic yells over his shoulder.

As the helicopter lifts off the ground, Brett looks at Gabby's pale face. His eyes fix on the oxygen mask and the intravenous fluids that are running into her veins. He closes his eyes and offers a prayer, "Please, let her live." Does she sense his plea or is it his imagination, as he thinks he sees her eyelids flutter? *Don't leave me, Gabby. You promised you would never leave.* His heart beats faster, pounding loudly in his ears. Taking a deep breath, he knows he must hold it together. She needs him to be strong. The family needs him to be strong.

The helicopter ride to the hospital is only a thirty-minute flight; however, Brett checks his phone at least a hundred times. He tries looking out the window at the land below, but his eyes dart back to Gabby as he searches for signs that she has regained consciousness.

After they land on the helipad, Gabby's stretcher is whisked away through the glass doors by the medical staff waiting for their arrival.

Brett paces back and forth in the hallway, wringing his hands. So much has happened over the past few hours, he is numb. He's grateful that Gabby's father, Wayne King, answered his call and was able to get the medivac helicopter on the way before Brett got her back to the ranch house. This may have saved the life of the woman he loves.

CHAPTER 2

As Brett walks to the side of the bed, he is intimidated by all the beeps and blips on the screens of the machines attached with their cords and tubes to Gabby. It's almost two in the morning now and she's been in this room in intensive care since she got out of surgery three hours ago. She looks frail in the hospital gown and the color of the sheets matches her white skin. Cautiously, he reaches out for her hand.

Once again, he sees her eyelids flutter ever so slightly.

"Hey, are you awake?" he asks, desperate to hear just one word to give him hope. "How do you feel?"

"Brett." Her voice is quiet and her eyes remain closed.

He runs his fingers through his hair with his other hand while he gives her hand a squeeze and then touches her cheek. He's shocked at how cool it feels.

"God, you scared me." He kisses her hand and she struggles to open her eyes. "You passed out in the Jeep. Then, you got a helicopter ride." He shifts his weight. "The doctors won't tell me anything more since I'm not family. They're waiting for your dad to arrive."

Her eyes are closed again and he isn't sure if she heard, but he needed to tell his story. If not, he feared he would explode. Her breathing is shallow and she seems to be sleeping so he leans over and kisses her, then pulls up a chair, ready to endure a long night. Nothing can keep him from being the first person she sees when she awakens. *I love you, Gabby. Hang in there.*

Sometime later, a noise makes him stir, but what? Brett looks around and it takes him a few seconds to remember. When his eyes adjust to the dim light, he sees a nurse looking at the numbers and wavy forms dancing on the monitor. She writes something on her clipboard.

"Sorry if I woke you," the nurse says softly.

"What time is it?"

"Almost six."

"Any changes?"

"For the past few hours, everything's pretty much the same. Her vitals are stable." As she tucks in the covers, she smiles at him. "It's a good sign."

When he looks at Gabby, he feels helpless. The numerous wires and tubes remind him of something from outer space. These things are all foreign. He watches the dark red liquid drip in the intravenous chamber and his eyes follow the tubing into Gabby's arm. The machines beep and buzz as if playing in a symphony, but this peculiar music is alien to his ears.

"I can tell how much you care. I think she's on her way to a full recovery," the nurse says. She walks to the door and turns to face him. "If you want to clean up, there's a shower down the hall. The docs will be making their rounds soon and then they'll be able to tell you more."

Brett stands and stretches. She flashes him a smile and pats him on the shoulder.

"Follow me. I'll get you a towel and a toothbrush."

She smiles at him again. The nurse is young and attractive. Brett wonders if she is this nice to all the visitors.

Taking a shower helps him wake up. The warm water running over his muscles feels good as they are cramped from sleeping in the chair. He must have nodded off for an hour or so. *Where is King? He should have been here by now.*

Freshly showered, he heads back down the hallway to the intensive care unit. As he approaches the double doors, the receptionist stops him.

"You need to sign in," the woman with the gray hair says, shoving a clipboard at him. "Who are you visiting?"

"Gabby King."

The woman looks down at the papers on her desk.

"Your name?"

"Brett Matthews." He reads her name tag—Maureen, volunteer. The receptionist cocks her head to the side. "And how are you related to the patient?"

"I'm her boyfriend...her fiancé."

He stares at the older woman. There must have been a shift change. The guard last night had no problems with him staying with Gabby. He needs to be by her side when she wakes up.

"I brought her in last night."

"Sorry, but you'll have to wait." She motions to the line of chairs and couches. "Take a seat."

"But I was with her all night." He knows that he has raised his voice from the hard expression on the volunteer's face.

"The doctors are making their rounds and the nurses need to do their work. Take a seat."

"I need to speak with the doctor," he pleads.

"I'm sorry, but you're not listed as family."

He shakes his head. "But I'm her fiancé.

"I follow the rules. Take a seat." This time her words are spoken with greater authority and she shoos him away before picking up the phone.

"Really?" he mutters as he turns, wondering if she was always this callous or if life made her hard and abrasive. Exhausted, he really doesn't want a confrontation. The last thing he needs is for her to call security and have him escorted out the doors. From her stern voice, he feels she isn't far from doing just that.

He walks into the waiting room but his nervous energy keeps him pacing back and forth. He needs to get to Gabby. Checking his cell phone, he sees a missed call from King.

Eagerly, Brett listens to the voice message: "Got to the hospital but you and Gabby were asleep. The doctor said that the bleeding has stopped and Gabby was stable from the drugs and blood infusion. Rita and I went on to our condo. We'll be there first thing in the morning. (Pause) Umm, Brett, thanks for taking care of my princess." He hears King's voice crack. "The doctors say that your quick thinking...may have saved her life."

Brett hangs his head and starts to shake. The realization of Gabby's close call with death brings tears to his eyes. He has been so strong these past eight hours. But, now, after hearing the confident Wayne King's emotional words, he feels that he is granted permission. The tears roll slowly down his cheeks and he doesn't wipe them away.

While he continues to pace back and forth, an elderly male volunteer approaches and offers Brett some coffee. Even though the white-haired volunteer doesn't talk, his kind face speaks volumes. The man hands him the cup and nods as though he understands. Brett wipes his face on the napkin and nods in return as the man leaves.

The black liquid rolls up the sides of the paper cup, almost spilling over the rim, telling Brett that he is still shaking; he wills his hand to be steady. Quickly, he brings the cup to his lips. The warm coffee slides down his parched throat, and it amazes him that something so simple makes him feel so much better. But was it the coffee, the cry, or the comradery of the kind volunteer?

CHAPTER 3

The intensive care waiting room doors open and King and his wife, Rita, hurry through. Brett paints on a smile, but his watery, emerald green eyes tell a different story. Sensing his pain, Rita hugs him so hard that their bodies rock back and forth as if doing a rehearsed dance. He buries his face in her hair, relieved to share with another who cares.

King returns after speaking with the older woman at the desk.

"The doctor is with her now," King says. "She'll come out and talk with us. Afterwards, we can go in, but only two at a time."

He gives Brett an embrace and pats him on the back. "Thank you, thank you. How are you, son?"

"Hanging in there, sir." He shifts his weight. "She's been sleeping. Her vitals have been stable for the past few hours. The nurse seems to think that the worst is over."

King flips his Stetson from one hand to the other. "Let's hope the doc tells us the same."

A few seconds later, a tall, middle-aged woman exits the ICU and approaches them. She is wearing blue scrubs, and a purple and blue surgical cap covers her hair, but strands of brown curls fall at the nape of her neck.

"Mr. King, Mrs. King," she says, while giving Brett a nod. "Hi, I'm Dr. Stevens. Your daughter was in pretty bad shape when she got here, but after giving her several pints of blood and the D and C—"

Aware of the puzzled expressions on all three faces, the doctor explains, "That's a surgical procedure. The sharp pain Gabby was experiencing was the placenta prematurely separating from the uterine lining. It's a very vascular area causing the patient to hemorrhage." The doctor scans them for signs of comprehension. "We didn't find a heartbeat for the fetus, so the baby probably died shortly after the bleeding first presented. At this early age of gestation, chances are fairly small that it could have survived, even if there had been a heartbeat." The doctor looks at Brett. "I'm so sorry."

"Does Gabby know?" Brett asks quickly.

Stevens pinches her lip. "I just told her. It'll take time for her to digest everything that has happened." After a pause, she says, "Gabby will go through the stages of grief. There will be denial and anger, then depression, before she reaches the acceptance stage. I can recommend a therapist." The doctor writes something on her notepad.

"My best advice for you is to surround her with love and be patient." Stevens turns to Brett and continues. "It could take a few weeks or a few months, but she'll come to terms with the loss, and many women are successful in getting pregnant within a few months when it is safe to try again. Gabby's young and she's healthy."

"Those things are in her favor," Rita chimes in as she strokes Brett's arm.

"One more thing," Stevens says. "Gabby has requested to see her baby. I think it would be a good idea if someone is with her. For many women, this difficult act helps them come to terms with the death." The doctor glances away as if looking back through the critical care doors. "Physically, she is doing great, so I wrote the order to move her to a regular room, and I'll discharge her tomorrow if her hematocrit level is normal. Any questions?"

Brett looks to King and Rita.

"Call me if you need anything. I have a surgery so I need to finish my rounds." The doctor turns and leaves through the same door that she entered.

King is the first to break the silence that fell among the small group.

"That's good news. Gabby will be fine. What a relief." He wipes his brow.

Placing her arm around her husband, Rita says, "Even though losing the baby is heartbreaking, the doctor said that Gabby can try again soon. It will all work out." Brett meets her eyes before turning away.

"Someone should be with her when she sees the baby." Rita touches his arm. "Are you up for that?"

His eyes shift from Rita to King and back again.

"I know Gabby loves me, but I think she would rather have you there." He nods at King. "She was so happy to give you a grandson. She would go on and on about all the things that you could teach him. I think you by her side would be best."

King places his arm around the younger man's shoulders and pulls him close. "I can do that. Yes, I think it would be best. Rita, let's go see our daughter."

"Since only two people are allowed at one time, why don't you and Brett go first? Go on." She rubs Brett's arm and nudges him toward the critical care unit. "You two go. I'll place a call to Jamie and Rusty. They must be so worried after seeing Gabby leave the ranch in the helicopter. I promised them an update."

She pulls out her cell phone to call the Joneses, the couple who are like kin to the King family as they have managed the ranch for more than twenty years. King checks with the receptionist. Maureen, the stern volunteer, stares at Brett. This time, he holds his head high, feeling an entitlement as he follows King through the double doors. How dare she think of stopping him now that he is in the company of the most admired oil man and cattle rancher in all of Texas?

When they enter the glass door to Gabby's room, she is staring out the window. If she heard them enter, she makes no attempt to acknowledge her visitors.

King sits on the bed and takes his daughter in his arms; he doesn't seem to be intimidated by all the medical equipment. Gabby buries her tear-streaked face in her daddy's chest. Sensing their shared love, Brett feels like an outsider.

"I'm so sorry, kitten. We almost lost you." He brushes her hair out of her face. "First, your mother, and now the baby—I thank God that you are still here with me."

"It just isn't fair. It isn't fair," Gabby cries.

"Life isn't fair. It just happens. I can't explain why God chose to take your little one. I'm so sorry, darlin'." King smooths her blond hair. "Hey, kitten, Brett's here."

She doesn't look up. At the mention of his name, Brett moves closer to the bed. He reaches for Gabby's hand.

"I'm so sorry, Gabby. You gave us quite a scare."

He feels better after she squeezes his hand in return. Brett shifts his weight and scratches his head. At a loss for more words of comfort, he says, "I'll get Rita. She's waiting outside."

"Back so soon?" Rita asks as she looks over the rim of her glasses.

"Rita, she doesn't even look at me." He hangs his head. "She doesn't talk to me and I don't know what to say. It's so awkward."

"Don't worry. You said it earlier, that girl needs her daddy right now. I'm going to give them more time alone." She pats the bench beside her. "Sit down and tell me all about last night. Start at the beginning, I want to hear every detail."

"It seems like last night was a decade ago. So much has happened."

Rita takes his hand. "So tell me. Take your time."

He shakes his head and takes a deep breath. "Everything was perfect—the evening breeze, the picnic. She was so excited to share the plans for our house." His voice becomes almost jovial. "She wants to build a tennis court, right there, in the back yard." Giving a little chuckle, he looks up. "She asked me to marry her. Did you know that?" He searches Rita's face and her approving nod makes him breathe a bit easier.

"Everything was going great. And then...and then, it all went to hell." He shakes his head and looks at his hands. "She was in so much pain. I could see the terror in her eyes. There was blood everywhere. I didn't know what to do. I didn't know..." His voice cracks and he starts to shake.

Rita takes him in her arms. "Hush, hush...it's okay. You did know what to do. You thought to ask for the medivac. You saved her life."

King is still holding Gabby in his arms when the nurse enters.

"If you're ready, Miss King, I'll bring in your baby."

She nods and sits straighter in the bed.

After the nurse leaves, King squeezes his daughter's hand. "You don't have to do this. You know that, right? It will be hard."

"I need to see him, Daddy." She hesitates just a few seconds as if in deep thought. "I saw him once already." She glances out the window before turning back to see King's puzzled face. His wide-eyed stare is a clue that he must think her mad, and she gives a small laugh before going on. "I held him in my arms...my sweet little boy. I touched him, smelled him, kissed him, and I felt his breath on my cheek. It was so wonderful." She sits straighter and pulls her shoulders back.

"I know you think I'm crazy, but it happened." Her voice is stronger now. "And when he looked at me, his eyes, they reminded me of you. His little hand grabbed onto my finger and he held on so tightly." She chokes back her sobs. "He was so beautiful. I'll never forget." She looks at her daddy's face, hoping he has marveled at what she said, but his troubled stare speaks volumes and she realizes he is uncomfortable.

She needed to share to validate her experience and to give words to the emotions swirling around inside her head. It was real, and she will always cherish that precious moment. She doesn't care that others may say it was merely a dream or an overactive imagination—something she created in her desperate need to feel better. She had held her baby, and what is more important is that Jacob will know her as his mother.

Her thoughts are interrupted as the nurse enters and pulls the curtain for privacy. A small bundle rests in her arms. "He only weighs a pound." she says as she opens the blanket that is covering the tiny face.

King stands and takes the baby. Even though he could easily hold Jacob in one hand, he handles the bundle as if it contains a piece of fine porcelain. He nods in Gabby's direction with sad eyes that seem to ask, "Are you sure you want to do this?"

As she holds out her arms, she notices that a lone tear has escaped and rolled down her daddy's cheek. He is crying.

Taking her son from King, she is shocked to find a small, blue, wrinkled face. Jacob looks more like an old man who has aged way before his time. She pushes back the blanket to expose the miniature arms and hands. She finds his hands small, as she remembers them bigger the first time they met. She kisses his tiny blue fingers and his cheek. Is this really Jacob? This is not what she remembers. The coldness of his skin is alarming, and her eyes begin to water. Distressed, she holds him away from her bosom. Everything is so different now.

Meanwhile, Rita and Brett have entered the room with the hospital chaplain. The chaplain takes Jacob from her outstretched arms.

"Gabby, Brett and I came to meet Jacob," Rita says. "The chaplain's here. He can anoint Jacob. Would you like that?"

After a few seconds pass, King pipes up, "Yes, that is a wonderful idea. Okay, kitten?"

She stares at the small assembly that has gathered, but she doesn't really see them. Brett walks to the other side of the bed to stand close to her and touches her shoulder. The chaplain is talking but the buzzing noise in her head keeps her from hearing his words. There are many voices talking simultaneously, creating confusion. Her earlier pleasant memories of her baby dim, and she fights to keep them from fading altogether.

The chaplain hands Jacob to Rita and then opens his prayer book. "Please state the name of the child."

Brett clears his throat. "Jacob Wayne King."

The ceremony is brief and it is as if Gabby is a distant spectator. She sees the chaplain's mouth moving but she doesn't hear any words. However, when he makes the sign of the cross, she is reminded of her own trinity. The new trinity composed of Brett, Gabby and Jacob is broken before it ever got started. Looking down at her wrist, she notices that her trinity knot bracelet is gone. It was a recent gift from Brett that represented their new family of three. Then she realizes that Jacob is gone.

"Where is Jacob?"

King says, "The nurse took him, kitten."

"But why?" Gabby's eyes are wide.

"It's for the best," King replies.

"No, bring him back. Tell her to bring him back."

"Jacob's gone, honey. He's no longer here with us."

"Bring him back." She swings her legs off the bed. "I need to see him."

"You have all of these wires and the IV," Brett says. "You can't get up." He gently places her legs back on the bed.

"Let me up!" she yells, pushing him away.

"Gabby, be reasonable."

"I'll be reasonable." She rips the IV out of her arm and the blood spills on the white sheets. *I must see Jacob. Why are they keeping me from my son?*

Brett grabs her arm and applies pressure to stop the bleeding, as he has seen at the rodeo when a thrown cowboy had the misfortune of getting speared by a bull's horns.

Rita shakes her head. "I'll go and get the nurse."

Gabby starts to hit Brett's arm away. *Why is he keeping me from Jacob?*

"Please, Gabby. Jacob isn't here." King tries to comfort her but she pushes him away. "Jacob is with God. I know it's hard for you."

"I need to see Jacob." Her screams are louder. Her hysteria is alarming.

"That's enough, Gabby," King says in his most authoritative, commanding voice.

Everyone falls silent, and Gabby is wide-eyed. Did her father just scold her? Did he raise his voice? She knows that if her daddy speaks harshly, the person on the other end deserves his response. He hasn't spoken to her in that tone in many years. Her shoulders slumping, she weeps as her upper body shakes with her gut-wrenching cries.

"I'm so sorry, kitten." King taps his Stetson against his leg and in a quiet tone filled with sorrow, he says, "Jacob is with God. He's not with us anymore." After nodding to Brett, he leaves the room.

Brett's arms cradle Gabby's limp body as the nurse redresses the IV site. The room is quiet. No one would ever guess the outburst that happened here just a few moments ago.

Finally, Gabby mutters, "Why did God take my baby?"

Brett holds her. "I don't know. I don't have any answers. But we'll get through this. Somehow, some way, together we'll get through this."

CHAPTER 4

Brett turns the key unlocking the door to Gabby's condo, flicks on the light and surveys the neat rooms. Her cheery place has always given him positive vibes and a feeling of happiness. He is hopeful he will not be disappointed tonight. Exhausted and hungry, he opens the fridge but only finds the fixings for salad and some fruit. He grabs an apple and shakes his head. *Women*, he thinks. *I need some real food.* Picking up his cell, he punches the number for the local pizza joint. He craves something meaty, greasy and considered sinful. Checking the time, he realizes if he hurries, he can shower before the delivery boy arrives.

After his shower, he buries his nose into the clean sweats and inhales deeply before putting them on. Yes, he has showered and the clothing is fresh, but he still feels dirty. He could not scrub away his sin. Making his way down the hall back to the living room, he reaches for the whiskey bottle and pours some over the ice cubes already in the glass. The loud crackling of the ice alerts him to the silence.

His mind takes him back to the moment on the ranch when, in the silence of the night, he heard the howl of a lone coyote. It was that haunting howl that gave him the courage to change his life's direction and ask Gabby to commit to their relationship. He was so carefree before meeting her—many would say that he was selfish and reckless. But was he happy? At least, he didn't hurt. He might have felt the twinge of loneliness now and then, but it was nothing compared to the sting of guilt that sits heavy on his shoulders tonight.

It is true that he wanted to be part of a family, but he didn't fathom that he was signing up for all this heartbreak. These past few months, since he stood on that porch listening to the sounds of the Texas night, have brought many changes in his life. He has dealt with hurt and disappointment, but there were also moments of joy and fellowship. He takes a swig of the whiskey and shakes his head. Is it worth it, this family thing, the commitment?

This spring, he had been devastated when Gabby left for the East Coast and even more upset upon learning that she was pregnant. Over time, he came to terms with the idea of fatherhood, but soon thereafter he learned that Richard, Gabby's previous boyfriend, was the father. However, Brett's love for Gabby ran deep and he wanted to keep her in his life, so he consented to raise the baby as his own.

Working through that was hard but he did it, and now with the death of the baby, his burden is lightened because Gabby's connection to Richard is broken. Does this make him a bad person?

The ringing of his cell phone startles him.

"Brett, come over for dinner," Rita says. "You must be hungry. You didn't eat anything today."

"Thanks, but I'm gonna stay here. I'm tired."

"Okay, honey, but if you change your mind, come over any time. There'll be leftovers."

"Thanks again, Rita, but I'm gonna hit the sack early."

"You still should eat."

"I ordered pizza. It'll be here in a few minutes." Brett looks over his shoulder at the clock.

"All right, I'll see you in the morning. Brett, you did good today, real good."

Once again, he stands in silence. *I did good today? Yeah, right? Oh, Rita, if you only knew how terribly guilty I feel.*

Quickly he empties his glass and pours another. His guilt has turned into shame. He is relieved that he's released from sharing the role of fatherhood with Richard, but he told Gabby a lie. He lied when he told her that he could love Jacob. Did God take Jacob because God, the omniscient God, knew that Brett could never be the father Jacob would have needed him to be?

Hanging his head, he recalls how King acted more like a father to Jacob than he. Brett didn't hold the baby—didn't even touch him. Wouldn't a real father have held his son and said goodbye? Once again, the memory of the coyote's howl haunts him. Maybe he was meant to be alone. Brett inhales a slice of pizza and washes it down with more whiskey.

Did he just refer to Jacob as his son? Maybe he could have loved him. A sense of calm hovers, his breathing slows, and he stands tall. Was that thought a wave of relief that washed over him, or was it the numbing effects of the whiskey that caused him to pull back his shoulders? God has spared him the fear of sharing paternity with Gabby's ex-boyfriend. Besides, being grateful after the fact doesn't make Brett a bad person, right? Jacob is gone. Nothing can change that.

Thinking about Richard always leaves a bad taste in Brett's mouth. He swirls the amber liquid around in the glass and bites his inner cheek. Brett despises Richard. The two men have a history of sharing serious words on several occasions, with Gabby always the cause of these confrontations. Richard had his chance. Even though he was a wealthy and a successful attorney, Gabby chose Brett instead.

"You lost, Richard," he says aloud and shoves another bite of pizza into his mouth. The corners of his mouth turn upward. Yes, many an eyebrow was raised when the news spread around the club that Gabby was dating their swanky, flirty tennis professional. But that's all in the past. Just this summer, Brett quit his job at the club and now works as a ranch hand on Wayne King's 300,000-acre ranch. Grateful to return to his roots, he is more content and happier than he has been in years. In addition to all that, he has found love.

Taking the last of the magical liquid, he closes his eyes. This numbness that now engulfs him feels much better than the previous self-pity. He pulls in a long deep breath and welcomes this inner peace that has crept in like the evening fog over a valley. Maybe God has granted him absolution. Is it possible that he can forgive himself?

CHAPTER 5

Gabby is aware of the sun's rays beaming through the hospital window only because the glare causes her to squint. Earlier this morning, the nurse asked her to walk the halls, encouraging her with orders that the doctor will not discharge her unless she completes all of the instructions.

She stands and catches a glimpse of herself in the wall mirror. Her hair is in desperate need of a shampoo and she fails to recall when her skin was this pale. Not that it matters. Nothing really matters anymore. She is tired with an overwhelming fatigue, one that she has never experienced before. Her sleep last night was broken, as she remembers waking in a sweat after having weird dreams filled with bizarre and grotesque images. She hangs her head, crosses her arms, and rubs her shoulders in an attempt to caress away the chills that those images bring.

As Gabby carefully toddled down the brightly lit hallway earlier, the nurse smiled; however, it was a costly mistake that the nurse didn't warn her that she would pass the nursery window if she continued in this direction.

When she reached that window, she stood in earshot of the excited chatter of the proud mothers gathered there. Her heart sank lower in her chest, making it difficult for her to breathe, but she refused to cry. All her tears were replaced with a dark emptiness.

Directly in front of the window, one of the mothers tried to strike up a conversation. Pretending not to hear, Gabby took a few steps farther away and was grateful the young mother didn't pursue her.

Gabby didn't know how long she watched the tiny blue and pink bundles in their plastic bins; however, eventually their numbers decreased as the nurses took the little ones to their mothers' rooms. Then she stood alone until a worker dressed in scrubs accompanied Gabby back to her room. She wasn't sure who the worker was—a nurse, a tech, a volunteer? The worker chatted and chatted, but Gabby only nodded in response. The same question went round and round inside her head louder than any voice from outside. "Why did God take my baby?"

The sound of Brett's voice sends shivers down Gabby's spine.

"Sorry if I startled you." He fidgets. "I said 'hello' twice. You must be in deep thought." He leans down to kiss her on the lips. "Care to share?"

She offers him her cheek instead, not aware that his smile fades.

"Are you ready to go home?" he asks, still leaning in close, trying to get the response he desires.

She glances up into his sparkling green eyes and wonders how he can be so cheerful. *I know he loves me and he's trying to make light of this horrible thing that has happened.*

Giving up on the kiss, he stands and looks out of the window. "It's getting hot. Rita is bringing your things—clothes and shoes." He runs his fingers through his curly brown hair. "I had no clue of what you would need. I was glad she offered to help." With no response to his initial question, he asks, "How do you feel?"

"Awful." Her voice is a soft whisper.

"Should I get the nurse? Are you in pain?" He sits on the edge of the bed and squeezes her hand.

She looks out of the window again. "No, no pain...just empty... and confused..."

"That's not a surprise after everything that has happened. Gabby, you almost died...and the baby..." He bites his lip and quickly turns away.

Her brow creases. *Maybe he is hurting too.* She strokes his arm. "Tell me about that night. How I got here...please."

He takes a deep breath and releases it through pursed lips.

"I can't seem to remember. What happened?" Her eyes beg and she tugs on his hand.

With the memory of her outrage over Jacob still fresh in his mind, can Brett tell her the events leading up to her hospitalization without upsetting her? He'd rather hold her and love her than rehash the trauma of that night. He doesn't want to add to her sadness but since he is the only witness, if anyone is to tell her, he would be the one. She does have the right to know, and maybe knowing about

27

that terrible night will stop her confusion and narrow the awkward gap that has widened between them.

Turning to face her, he says, "Tell me what you remember and I'll fill in the gaps, okay?"

She nods in agreement. "We were by the lake having a picnic. I was wearing my new green dress, the one that matches your eyes."

Her voice grows more confident with each sentence. "We were so happy."

He smiles. *Yes, this is working better than I thought.*

She closes her eyes. "And I asked you to marry me...and you said, 'Yes.'" She opens her eyes and scans his face.

"I sure did. I made you ask me twice. Remember?" He smiles as he pushes a loose strand of blond hair off her face.

"There were lights. Yes, the twinkling fairy lights were hanging from the large old oak." Her voice drifts off.

He waits a few seconds. "Do you remember the plans for our house...the tennis court?"

She nods. "And we picked a name...Jacob, after your father." Her eyes fill with tears. "Then what happened? I can't remember. What happened?" She pulls on his arm.

Looking into her eyes, he finds a frightened stare. "Gabby, you okay?" He reaches out to calm her shaking.

With an unsteady voice she says, "I'm not sure. There's this big, black, black hole. I can't remember."

"Maybe it's too soon. You're shaking like a leaf. I'll go get a nurse."

She pulls on him with both arms. "Don't go. Please, I need to know what happened to me. Tell me. Please, you must tell me."

"Hey, move over." He sits on the chair and cuddles her in his lap.

Still shaking, she leans into his chest. She squeezes his firm bicep and gives a long sigh.

He gently rocks her. This started so positively. In the beginning, they even shared a smile. Now this. Relieved that her shaking is lessened, he wants to stop, to cease the telling, but he has misinterpreted her silence.

"Well, what happened next?"

Her persistence makes him inhale deeply. It is against his best judgment to continue.

With as little emotion as possible he recounts the events of that night as if he is reading a grocery list. "You had bleeding and then you passed out. That's why you can't remember. You were unconscious. I carried you to the Jeep and called your dad, asking him to get the medics. They brought you here."

"I don't remember," she says faintly.

"Of course you don't remember, honey. You were unconscious." He strokes her hair. His emotions get the best of him and his matter-of-fact voice disappears. "I was so scared. I was afraid that I lost you." He holds her tight and kisses the top of her head. She buries her face deeply into his chest.

"They let me ride along. The doctors let me stay right by your bed in ICU. Do you remember that? You spoke to me."

She looks up at him. "I did?"

"Yes, you did." He hugs her again.

"I don't remember. I want to remember. It would help to remember. Remembering would be better than this big hole...this big hole of blackness. I want to remember Jacob."

She sits up and her eyes are wild, darting back and forth as if she is searching for something that has tumbled down into a dark space.

"Hey, I'm here. You're safe now. I know it hurts, Gabby. It'll just take time. It has only been a day," he says gently, and she falls back against his body.

"I'm so tired."

She reminds him of a small child who is seeking comfort in her daddy's lap. Did he ease her pain? She is quiet in his arms with her eyes closed.

"Hey, you two." Rita pokes her head into the hospital room, smiling. Gabby stirs in Brett's lap. King and Rita stand in the doorway arm in arm, radiating happiness. After taking a job at Rita's art gallery in Austin, Gabby had introduced her daddy to Rita, and they were married just a few short months ago.

Rita unzips the blue bag that she carries and places it on the bed. "I brought two different sizes." She holds up the dresses that she pulled out. "I didn't know which would fit. I also brought you a brush and some makeup."

Gabby stares but doesn't respond. King stands near the chair where Brett and Gabby sit.

"Hello, kitten." Gabby looks up but doesn't speak so he continues, "I think it's best for you to come to our condo for a few days...until you're back to your old self. How does that sound?" He looks to Rita for support. "Rita and I need to stay here in town for a bit."

"No," Gabby says. "I want to go to my condo. My things are there. Brett can stay with me."

"Tell us what you need and we'll get it for you." King taps his Stetson hat with his nervous fingers. "Honey, Rusty needs Brett back at the ranch. We're getting the cattle ready for market. Besides, Brett needs to practice for the rodeo." He paces back and forth and glances at Brett as though in search of confirmation.

"I want to go home." Her voice is whiny.

"Gabby, you shouldn't be alone right now. Please stay with us." Rita moves closer to King. "It's only for a few days."

Brett sits up straighter in the chair and scans the determined faces. He squeezes Gabby's hand. "Gabby, will you consider recuperating at the ranch?" He then focuses his attention on King. "Sir, would that be okay with you? The doctor said that the threat of more bleeding is over. Ummm...I can work during the day and Jamie can help watch Gabby, and then I'll be there in the evening. You can stay here in town, get your work done. Jamie and I can take care of Gabby." He squeezes her hand again. "Hey, what do you think?"

She looks out of the window before answering in a soft voice, "I can do that."

Brett notices that her tone is flat and distant, but things will get better when he can get her out of this dreadful place. He is certain of it.

"Yes, I think that will work. I need Brett at the ranch, and Jamie makes an excellent nurse. Good." King claps his hands together. "You can stay at your place tonight and drive out to the ranch tomorrow. The cattle won't wait. So you need to get on the road at an early hour. I'll call Jamie so she can prepare for your visit, and Rusty will be grateful that his prize cattle cutter will be working the herd."

Brett shifts his weight in the chair and smiles.

"Gabby, I'll tell Rusty that Brett will be there by nine a.m.," King says in a commanding voice. "Brett, let's you and me get a coffee. Our two lovely ladies can get things moving so we can all exit this joint." He taps Rita on the butt with his Stetson.

"Wayne." Her face turns red as she pushes his hand away.

Brett lifts Gabby from his lap and places her on the bed, then plants a quick kiss on her lips. "You heard the boss. See you later."

King turns at the doorway. "Text me when you're ready and I'll meet you in the front with the car."

Rita smiles back at Gabby, "You heard your daddy. Let's get you out of here!" Rita holds up a sunny, blue-and-yellow flowered dress. "You can try this one on first."

Reluctantly, Gabby stands, removes her hospital gown and allows Rita to place the dress over her head.

"There, it will do. It's not the most flattering but it'll get you home." Rita zips up the back of the dress and turns Gabby to face her. "I know it's tough. I know you're sad. It'll just take time, honey. You've suffered a terrible loss. Come here." Rita pulls her in close and embraces her for a few seconds, but Gabby stiffens and keeps her arms close to her side.

Breaking the awkward tension, Rita says, "Now, that hair, we have to do something about that hair. My, oh my, what a mess! Sit down here." She pats the chair by the window. "You're too tall. Sit."

With each stroke of the brush as it travels down her long blond locks, Gabby is reminded of Anna, her mother. Those days are long in the past, as Anna died when Gabby was a senior in high school. Now, she closes her eyes and recalls her childhood.

Gabby would stare at her mother through the reflection in the vanity mirror, wishing that she would grow up to be as beautiful. Anna would take the large silver brush, engraved with bluebonnets, and run the bristles through her wavy auburn hair.

On a rare occasion, Anna would motion for Gabby to sit on her lap. While brushing her daughter's hair, Anna would tell stories about her childhood. Young Gabby would sit and listen intently to the words describing her mother's life on the ranch. She enjoyed learning about her grandparents and her uncles. Her mother spoke about how hard they worked without having the convenience of electricity and running water. She spoke of her father's encounters with the Indians as he was out herding cattle.

Sometimes her mother would scold, "Gabby, stop squirming. How did you get your hair so tangled? If you're going to be playing by the creek, you need to wear a cap. Those sycamore trees and cedars are filled with spiderwebs and worms."

In her mother's vanity drawer was a black-and-white photo, yellowed with age, showing a stern-looking couple. Anna explained to her that in days long past, it was customary not to smile for pictures. She thought that strange as this was her grandparents' wedding photo. Shouldn't they look happy? She also thought it strange that her grandmother did not wear a white lace dress or carry a bouquet of flowers. Things were definitely different back then.

Where is that photo? She will need to look for it when she is at the ranch later this week. Her daddy made a point of stressing how badly Brett was needed back at the ranch. She can't find fault with that as she is aware the fall season is a busy time. The cattle need to be herded and sent to market and there is much preparation for the cold months ahead. Besides, it might be good for her to spend some days recuperating at the ranch. Being close to her roots may help ground her. Ground...roots...the family cemetery. It didn't occur to her that she would have to...A shiver sweeps over her.

"Gabby, are you feeling all right?" Rita puts down the brush.

Gabby shakes her head and shudders as if chasing her thoughts away.

"Should I get the nurse?"

"No, no, I just felt a draft," she lies. Aware that her eyes would betray her, she turns, pretending to look out of the window. The thoughts return. *Jacob, dear Jacob, he is not alone. My mother will take care of him.* A smile as gentle as that of the Mona Lisa crosses her lips. *Yes, precious Jacob is with my mother, and he will make those two serious people in that yellowed photo smile.* She closes her eyes and pinches her lips tight.

"Gabby, you didn't hear a word I said, did you?" Rita touches her on the shoulder. "It doesn't matter. I was just rambling on. There, that looks much better. You're so pretty. What was I thinking, bringing this makeup." She gathers up the small compact and lipstick and places them in the bag. "You look great."

Rita steps back and wrings her hands. "I shouldn't have said that—not after what you've been through. I'm really sorry, Gabby, but you know what I mean. I'll go and tell the nurse you're ready."

Rita heads out the door. "Check around, dear, make sure we have everything."

Gabby stands and looks around the hospital room, well aware that she is missing something, something very precious. The constant empty feeling deep in her soul does not let her forget. Covering her face with her hands, she lets out a long sigh, and the warmth of her breath makes her notice her cold hands. Breathing in deeply, she raises her head and her hands fold as if in prayer. "Please, God, help me get through this pain. It is more than I can bear alone."

The sun's rays dance in the room in an attempt to create a sense of cheeriness; however, it will take more than the sun has to give to fill the dark hole carved into her heart.

CHAPTER 6

Gabby reads the lines of instructions on the papers given to her at discharge again, referring to them as "the rules," and rolls her eyes. In the two weeks since she was discharged from the hospital, she's looked at them several times each day and should have them memorized.

No swimming for four weeks. No sexual intercourse for four weeks. No lifting more than ten pounds. No strenuous activity—no horseback riding is written in ink after this one. Report any increased bleeding. Call the office for a follow-up appointment.

Sitting next to the paper is a small brown bottle. Gabby picks it up and reads the label before removing the white cap. *Take one every 4-6 hours as needed.* She dumps a mound of the oval-shaped, peach-colored pills into her hand. Fingering each one gently, she returns them to the bottle. Are these pills making her feel so flat? She's been told that she needs her rest, but she seems to sleep most of the day. *What day is today, anyway?* She's not sure as all of the days seem to run together. They are all the same—get up, shove down some breakfast, take a shower, then take a nap. Wake up, get dressed or not, have a few bites of lunch, only because she needs to ward off a lecture from Jamie about how she must eat to gain back her strength. This is followed by another nap.

But always, always, she takes her little pill, allowing the numbness to settle in. She has tried reading, but she can't concentrate and within minutes, she's asleep. She can't remember the last time she's cried. Crying would take energy. She hasn't attempted to wander out of the house. That too would require too much effort. She puts the bottle down and looks at her reflection in the mirror on the dining room wall. *Who is this person? Look at that drawn face and those dark circles under my eyes. God, I'm a mess. I'm not doing this anymore.*

Over toward the window in the corner is her easel. Several days ago Jamie had placed a drop cloth and set Gabby's tripod with a blank canvas next to her painting supplies. In the past, she had found her voice through her art, and it could work this time as well. She had painted through her grief over Anna's death with her Trinity Knot series, and she had painted her joy over her father's marriage to Rita with the Zeppelin Bend. Lastly, she painted The Hitch, a painting she presented to Brett the night she asked him to marry her. *The night of...*She shudders. *I can't go there. And poor Brett, how does he put up with me? I haven't been very nice to him, have I? And he has been through so much. It's selfish to think that I am the only person who has suffered a loss.*

All of this thinking causes her shoulders to droop. She's tired, so tired that her insides have stopped screaming her pain. Rubbing her forehead, Gabby comes to an understanding. *I would rather hurt than this nothingness.* A second later, she hurls the bottle across the room and the oval tablets scatter over the wooden floor.

"Gabby, what was that?" Jamie yells, running out of the kitchen and wiping her hands on her apron.

Looking from the mess on the floor to Jamie and back down again, Gabby answers, "I'm sorry. I'll pick them up." She gets down on her knees.

"Hey, I'll fetch the broom. You shouldn't be doing that." Jamie firmly places her hands on Gabby's shoulders. "You're right to throw them away. I know, doctor's orders and all that, but I hate what they are doing to you."

Letting a handful of pills she had gathered roll to the floor, Gabby stares up with wide eyes. This is not the reaction she thought she would receive.

Jamie takes Gabby's hands in her own. "I know that it hurts. It hurts like hell. No pill is going to take that away. I know that pain. I lost a child once. Here, let me help you up."
Gabby cocks her head to the side but allows Jamie to assist her to stand.

"I don't talk about it much. It happened a long time ago." Jamie draws in a deep breath. "I was a young girl, younger than you are now. Rusty and I were only married a few months." Jamie turns her face away as if she is unable to allow Gabby to find the deep scar hidden behind her green eyes.

"I had what they called an ectopic pregnancy. At the time, I had no idea what they were telling me, but it seems that the baby lived in my fallopian tubes. When it burst, I lost the tube and my ovary. Next, came the infection and then, well...I just could never have children."

She squeezes Gabby's hands. "But you, my precious one, you will be able to have another baby. I know that doesn't make this loss any easier, but you'll heal and I pray to God that he will bless you with many children."

Gabby lowers her eyes. "Oh, Jamie, I'm so sorry."

"Hush, child, I didn't tell you this so that you would feel sorry for me. I told you so you would know that you're not alone. I understand, and masking your pain with those drugs just prolongs facing the harsh reality. It hurts. It hurts...but the pain will get further away with time."

Gabby is at a loss for words. She had always assumed that Jamie and Rusty never wanted children. She had no idea. In all of these years, she had never asked. *Poor Jamie.*

"You're like a daughter to me. You're the daughter that I wasn't able to have, and I thank God every day that he gave you to me. I am ever so grateful." Jamie turns toward the kitchen to get the broom and Gabby follows.

Returning to the dining room with the broom in her hand and Gabby still at her heels, Jamie sweeps. "First thing I would tell my daughter is to stop taking these pills. The side effects are worse than the depression. The second thing I would tell my daughter is to pick up her paintbrush and do what she does best." Jamie props her chin on the broom handle and nods toward the easel.

"Paint, Gabby, paint. No pill can do what that canvas can do for you. Best therapy ever, child, just paint."

Gabby leans into Jamie and gives her a hug.

"My sweet, sweet girl...this too shall pass. Give it time. Now—oh, my, oh, my—this floor sure is dirty, just nasty. Shame we have to throw these pills away." Jamie winks at her as she sweeps the mound of pills into the dustpan. "Perfect day for painting. See how the light is coming in the window." She nods toward the easel. "Let me know if you need anything."

Facing the easel, Gabby feels nothing. Moments pass as she sits, her eyes staring at the blank, white canvas. *I can't paint. Wait, what do I hear?* Music is coming from the overhead speakers. Jamie must have sensed that she needed some help. Beethoven's "Moonlight Sonata" is soothing and carries warm memories. At one time, she could play this piece on the piano. The familiar classical tune makes her pinch her lips together. Her mother would ask her to play this piece. Yes, that's when she stopped playing the piano. She stopped playing after Anna died.

The brief inner peace has been replaced with the familiar void, that sense of loss; however, can she take comfort that Anna and Jacob are together? She takes another deep breath and she is overcome by the heaviness that engulfs her. She cries.

Soon, the notes of the music begin to dance in Gabby's darkness and tug at her heart, begging her to partner with them. Each note is like a flicker of light, casting sparks of hope through the darkness. Follow the notes. Let them lead you, one step, now another, and again…

She doesn't remember the exact moment she picked up the brush, but she remembers humming to the sonata she loves and thinking of her family. She remembers the satisfying feeling of swirling the brush into the fresh paint that she squeezed out of the tubes. She remembers mixing the colors to create varying earth tones.

The music kept luring her out of her darkness. She could not resist the pleading of the notes and with the brush in her hand, she became their dance partner. At first, her steps were shy and timid. Her brush skimmed the surface of the canvas, barely leaving its mark. But as the music continued to engage her with its rhythm and melody, her brush strokes became more confident, together their strides were longer, and at last they were waltzing.

Now, she steps back and gazes at the canvas as she chews on the end of her paintbrush and tries to make some sense out of her spontaneous creation. The horizontal composition mimics a landscape. Scanning the painting from the bottom to the top, her eyes open wide and she sucks in her breath. The light, cream-colored, feathery brush strokes in front of her are like an angel's wings. However, instead of the wings lifting up toward heaven, they appear to be fluttering down as if visiting earth. Is Anna sending her a message? Is Jacob with her mother?

Closing her eyes, she bows her head and prays, "Thank you." Wiping her tears with her shirt, she isn't sure if they are tears of sorrow or tears of joy, but she's convinced that this is a sign. Although nothing can change the past, now as she paints, it is as if she can feel her mother's presence giving her an inner peace. Feeling encouraged with the brush in her hand, stroking the canvas, she continues to dance.

Hours later, Gabby stands and steps away from her work, viewing her painting from a distance. Her legs are tired. Her arms are tired. Her canvas echoes her exhaustion as her latest brush stokes appear more as smudges, instead of the joyful waltz that graced the canvas earlier. When did the music stop?

For the first time in almost a week, she strolls across the room, opens the front door and steps out unto the porch. The afternoon sun makes her squint, but its rays warm her soul. She throws back her shoulders, takes in a deep breath, filling her lungs with fresh air. *With time, everything will be all right.* It may not be today, or this week or even the next, but the act of painting has assured her that with time everything will be all right.

Jamie was a wise woman. The canvas is her therapist but also her friend. She told it her sorrows, her struggles, her joys, and her wishes. The canvas listened today, and more important than this, her canvas has given her answers.

PART II

CHAPTER 7

North Carolina

Stan Adams needs to feel free. He grips the throttle, pressing it harder. The engine roars as the machine beneath him comes alive, speeding like a rocket up the windy road. His large body mass leans the bike hard into the turn to maintain control and his eyes focus on the road ahead.

Stan usually works at the motorcycle mechanic shop on Saturdays, but this weekend the thirty-three-year-old bachelor took time off and has chosen to take his bike to the mountains on a sort of joy ride in an attempt to get that girl off his mind and out of his heart. His previous efforts haven't been successful, but now, he has hopes that this invigorating ride will do the trick. He started his adventure early in the morning, and his body is beginning to feel the effects of the ride. He rolls his shoulders to relieve some of the muscle tension from hunching over. Then he flexes his wrists. Why didn't he pull over at the scenic overlook a few miles back?

He grips the throttle again. Speeding around hairpin turns on his BMW is certainly exhilarating. He feels the sweat on his brow under his helmet.

After some research, the Blue Ridge Parkway seemed the most alluring and accessible ride since it was just a few hours from his home in Washington, D.C. He is headed to The Dragon, located at the southern end in North Carolina and claimed to be the best motorcycle road in the nation, famous for its three hundred curves in a short eleven miles.

Yet even on this beautiful fall day, and even with the head rush from the speed, his thoughts still migrate back to Gabby. All of the wishing in the world would not make her his. Lord knows, he certainly tried hard enough. He even tried the foolish gesture of wishing on a star, just like Gabby taught him. He had thought this silly, but anything to make her love him was worth a try. He needs to accept that their relationship wasn't meant to be and to move on, but it is still hard to swallow.

Gabby has made her choice. She is back in Texas and back in Brett's arms. Yes, life goes on and he must go on. However, it isn't that simple, because not only will he have to see his stepsister again, but he will have to see her with Brett. That image makes him bite his lip. There's no way to avoid it. It was just six months ago that Stan's mother, Rita, married Gabby's dad. That's when he and Gabby first met. He was lured by her long blond hair and deep brown eyes, smitten with her beauty at first glance.

Thinking of her, he lessens his grip on the throttle and the bike slows. He shakes his head. How did he get so messed up? Usually, he is more cautious but he remembers how it all started. It was the night of his mother's wedding out on the King ranch. That night, Gabby had stirred more emotion in him than any woman he had previously dated, and it was love. Well, at least for him. He remembers taking her in his arms and sharing a dance. He remembers the softness of her skin and her soft floral scent. And when the music stopped playing, he did not let go. He looked into her eyes and it was as if he found a piece of heaven. He shakes his head again to make the image go away. Hell, he's acting like a foolish, lovesick schoolboy, instead of a thirty-three-year-old man.

Falling in love with her was easy. He recalls her slender curves, high cheekbones, pouty lips, and lustrous hair. She is smart but her most redeeming quality is her kindness. Yes, Gabby King is the full package.

Why would a woman like her glance twice his way? His forehead was growing larger rather quickly and even though he was toned, he was only a few inches taller than she. She could have any man she wanted. He was a fool to think that she would consider him as a father to her unborn child. When he made the offer, he hoped to persuade her but she declined and chose Brett instead. It still hurts.

The road is winding up the mountain so he has gotten away with not concentrating one hundred percent on the job at hand, but when starting the descent he will need to focus on the ride, leaning into the turns at just the right angle. He rides to stop thinking about her and he's not succeeding. Sweat runs from his brow as the sun beats down on his black helmet and black leathers. Stan hunches over and pulls hard on the throttle causing the bike to rear up as he reaches the summit. At this faster speed he must concentrate. He needs to anticipate. *Gabby, go away.*

At the top of the mountain, the wind is pushing him. Even though he wants to pay attention, his mind refuses to obey and his thoughts keep racing.

Lately, his mother has phoned him frequently. This is unusual so he is sure that his brother, Will, has been whispering into her ear that he has been reclusive. He knows that she's just concerned. That's a mother's job but Stan doesn't want mothering. He wants Gabby.

Distracted by the scenario playing out in his head, he leans aggressively into the turn, unaware of a patch of gravel. The rear wheel of the bike flares out and he loses traction. With a surge of adrenalin, he hits the brake, causing the wheel to right itself. In an instant he high-sides and is airborne. The motorcycle jets downhill and slams into a pine tree. Everything goes black.

CHAPTER 8

He's alive. For that Stan is grateful and he takes a deep breath. He opens his eyes and squints from the glaring sun. What happened? Yes, now he remembers—the turn, going airborne, and the tree. He remembers the branches hitting hard into his helmet. Testing to see if he is paralyzed, he moves his neck and attempts to move his arms and legs.

Hot and sweaty, he wants to unzip the jacket. He winces in pain when attempting to lift his left arm to take off his gloves. "Shit," he mutters. *Damn, it may be broken but at least I can move.* He tries the other arm. *Good, this one is okay.* He removes his gloves and helmet with his right arm.

He can feel his legs but he can't move them as they are pinned under his bike. He is in so much pain, he feels dizzy. *Keep it together.* He takes some slow deep breaths and tries to collect his thoughts. *Don't focus on the pain.* The last thing he needs is to black out again.

He tries to wiggle out from underneath the massive machine but it's the biggest BMW makes, and he can't get free. His leg must be broken as the pain is excruciating. *This is not good. I will need help.* Reaching inside his jacket pocket with his right arm, he retrieves his cell phone and dials 911, then closes his eyes. His body starts to shake. He may be going into shock. *Damn it.*

"911, emergency." The operator's voice seems to be in a distant tunnel.

"Hey, Stan, is that really you?" Will leans his head inside the door peering around the hospital room. "How are you feeling, bro?"

Bedridden with his leg suspended in a sling, Stan motions Will to come in. With him is his petite brunette bride, Ella, and the newlyweds approach smiling, arm in arm. Their happiness reminds him of his woes. But before he can answer, Will says, "You look like hell."

Ella, standing on tiptoes, leans over and gives him a kiss on the cheek. She shakes her head at Will. "Honey, stop teasing. Stan feels bad enough."

"He knows I'm joking. Well...not really. You do look like hell. Hey, what's this?" Will taps the sling. The weight hanging over the end of the bed providing traction for the leg starts swinging back and forth and makes a thumping noise as it hits the bed frame.

"Ouch, why'd you do that?" Stan yells. "Don't touch anything,"

"Pussy," Will mocks. "Hey, look at this hardware. The size of that pin is incredible. Does it really go all the way through your leg?" He gets down at eye level and peers at the metal rod.

Stan rolls his eyes. "God, you're annoying. And, yes, it goes through. So like I said, don't touch anything."

"Okay, okay." Will pulls up a chair and sits next to the bedside, staring at his older brother. "You really did it this time."

Changing the subject, Stan gestures toward the package Ella is holding. "Is that for me?"
Seconds later he has both cheeks packed with homemade chocolate chip cookies. "Best thing, I've eaten in days. The food here sucks."

Ella reaches into her oversized purse and pulls out a small brown paper bag.
He cocks his head to the side. "You snuck in beer?" His smile is contagious.

"No, silly," Ella giggles. "It's not beer but you won't be disappointed." After opening the bag, she hands him the quart-sized bottle of milk and pulls a chair up next to Will.

Drinking straight from the bottle, Stan beams up at her with a white milk mustache.

"So, how long are you going to be in this joint?" Will asks.

"Another week or two. They can't put a cast on this until the bones align and until this cut heals. They want to make sure it's clean and healed before casting so I don't wind up with an infection." He pops another cookie in his mouth and follows it with a swig of milk.

"So, I get to lie here, watch TV, take drugs, and use this little button." He holds up the call light. "This is a chick magnet." He winks, then flashes a boyish grin. "All I have to do is push this button and beautiful women come to my room...sometimes two." He raises his eyebrows. "God, that bedpan, the worst thing ever invented." Stan shakes his head. "I don't understand why in the past one hundred years something a little more humane hasn't been invented."

"Maybe that's something you can do while you are waiting for the docs to put on that cast," Will says. "Hey, what are your plans after you get your cast? You go to a rehab center?

"Since I crushed the bones in my leg, I won't be able to bear weight for six weeks so I'll be in a wheelchair. I can't use crutches until this arm heals a bit." He holds up his casted right arm. "I'm hoping Mom will help. I don't want to go to one of those rehab places. In return for her generosity, I know she'll want me to swear that I'll never ride again." He sucks in a breath and bites his lip. "You know I can't do that."

"Even if she says that initially, she knows you love to ride. You know how Mom is, she'll get over it after you get back to normal," Will says.

"I don't know about normal. I may have a permanent limp. I'll get that 'I told you so lecture' from her."

"She'll get over it. Just having her son around to baby for a while will soften her. And you, bro, you'll use that famous Stan charm."

"This could have been a lot worse. If I had landed just a few feet farther down that mountain, nothing would have stopped me from falling down that cliff. I'm also lucky that I didn't break my neck. I could be paralyzed or dead." Stan's tone has changed from jovial to solemn.

"Maybe you should stop riding? What about your bike?"

"Totaled, I hear. It landed on top of me and after calling 911, I can't remember. Haven't seen her since and no one has called." Stan shifts his weight in the bed and says to Ella, "Can you move this pillow over a bit?"

Ella stands to assist him with the pillow. "Did you know Gabby's also at the ranch?" Her stare is piercing as if she is trying to see inside his head.

He looks away. *Damn, he just gave her the information she was seeking.* He peers out the hospital window. "Yeah, I heard. I'm sorry she lost the baby."

Will squeezes Ella's shoulders. "Ella has yet to share our news. We're not sure how Gabby will take it after everything she's been through." Stan turns his attention back to the couple and knits his brow.

"We can tell him, can't we?" Ella pulls on Will's arm.

"Ella's pregnant, Stan." Will points his finger at his brother. "You're going to be an uncle."

"Really? Wow, congratulations. That's wonderful, right?"

"We're happy about it. However, the timing sucks. I hate telling Gab." Ella looks down at her hands. "It's too soon. I want my best friend to be happy for me, not resent me."

"Gabby wouldn't do that. She'll be happy for you, for both of you." Stan smiles at Will. "Did you tell Mom?"

"Not yet, and we'd appreciate it if you kept our secret. We're giving everyone time to adjust. Ella and I don't wish to add to Gabby's grief."

"So how far along are you?" Stan looks from his brother back to Ella.

"Just a few months. Baby's due early spring." She pats her stomach.

"That's really great. I'm happy for you. I'm going to be an uncle!" He lifts his quart bottle of milk as if toasting.

CHAPTER 9

The King Ranch

Upon hearing Rita's heavy and hurried steps on the stairs, Gabby looks up from her canvas that she's been working on all morning. She can read alarm on her stepmother's face. She quickly puts down her brush and rushes toward Rita.

"What's wrong?" Gabby says.

Catching her breath, Rita wrings her hands and avoids looking at Gabby. "It's Stan, Gabby. He's hurt. He's really hurt." She draws her arms up to her chest.

"He's had an accident. I knew this day was coming. I told him when he first bought that damn motorcycle. I warned him that it was dangerous. But stubborn Stan, he refused to take it back." Rita paces back and forth and stares out of the window as she talks. "It happened more than a week ago." She throws her hands up in the air and turns to face Gabby. "Can you imagine that...a week ago? He said that Will has been to the hospital several times. Those boys, keeping something like that from their mother—and for a whole week. If I could, I would take them both over my knee."

Gabby doesn't dare interrupt and she stands back to give Rita more space in the living room.

"Now, he tells me. If he had only told me earlier, I could have flown to D.C., stood by his bedside and held his hand. Prayed for him." Rita paces back and forth. "I need to leave as soon as possible. I need to get there for my baby."

"Rita, stop for a minute and take a deep breath. Who called you?"

"Stan did, just now. You've spoken with Ella a few days ago—have you been keeping this from me too?"

"No, Ella never mentioned it. I'm really sorry. How did Stan sound?"

"He told me I would be angry. Well, he got that one right." She continues her pacing, shaking her head. "He even joked about it. Like this is something to joke about?"

"But that's a good sign, right, the joking? Tell me what he said."

"He was out riding his motorcycle somewhere in North Carolina. I can't remember where exactly. The whole situation upsets me so." She rubs her forehead. "Give me a minute."

"Come, sit down on the couch. Take a deep breath. Tell me everything." Gabby pats the cushion on the couch and motions toward her stepmother.

After taking a seat next to Gabby, Rita holds her head in her hands as she props her elbows on her knees. "I want to wring his neck. Wait 'til I get Will on the phone. He was in on all of this. Keeping his brother's secret."

"So Stan had an accident on his motorcycle in North Carolina,"

Gabby says. "And if he is calling you and able to joke about it, he must be on the mend."

"He broke his arm and his leg. It seems like his broken leg is the worst part. He remembers the accident but he doesn't remember anything that happened after he dialed 911. He says he was unconscious and woke up after the operation in a hospital bed in traction. He didn't even know what hospital or what state he was in. Can you imagine that?" She squeezes Gabby's hand.

"His leg has several broken bones. He's got pins holding it together but they are going to cast it tomorrow. If he does well, he'll be discharged in a few days. Thank God for that." She looks up as if in gratitude. "He'll have trouble getting around. With a cast on his arm, he can't use crutches. He'll be in a wheelchair for a while. He asked if I would mind helping him out a bit by having him stay here at the ranch." She stares into Gabby's eyes. "Of course, I'll take care of him. That's what family is for."

Gabby rubs Rita's back and is relieved that talking, along with a need to be helpful, has seemed to calm her. "Yes, Stan needs to come here. He loves the ranch and the fresh air will be good for him. I'll help you take care of him. He has done so much for me. I owe him." She pats Rita's hand. "Your sons didn't want to worry you. That's why they didn't tell you. They knew you would be upset."

"Of course I would be upset. He's my little boy."

Gabby looks down at her lap and bites her lip. She does understand all too well. Not wishing to dwell on that, she swallows hard. "When do you think Stan will be there?"

"He is thinking three days if all goes as planned. He wants Wayne to send a jet. I'll talk to your father."

"I'm sure Daddy will do whatever it takes. Stan is family and Daddy is big on family."

Rita looks at her sideways. "You said you're fine with Stan coming here, but how do you think Brett will feel? Those two men have a bit of a history. If I recall, they haven't seen each other since your art opening in Virginia. I thought they were going to have a fist-fight right there. It's a good thing Will was able to step in between them before any punches were thrown." Rita rolls her eyes. "It could be awkward."

"Under the circumstances, I'm sure Brett will understand...I'll talk to him. Like you said, Stan is family."

"With a broken arm and leg, it's not like Stan is going to be chasing after you," Rita quips as she stands. "I need to call Wayne and get this show on the road or rather the plane in the air. I need to pack."

Gabby follows Rita as she skips up the stairs. Things around here will be interesting. How is she going to tell Brett that Stan is coming to the ranch for a few weeks or maybe even months?

CHAPTER 10

Brett, why do you love me?

"I don't know...I just do."

"No, that isn't an answer. I really want to know. Why do you love me?"

He looks at her with a furled brow. "Come on, Gabby, I just do."

They are sitting on the glider on the porch, sipping iced tea. The house is quiet. Jamie is in the kitchen preparing dinner, and Rita and King had left earlier in the day, driving the two-hour trip to Austin to do some shopping. Earlier, Rita mentioned the need to buy some new furniture for the family room with an excuse that it would make things easier for Stan to get around. Well, that may be true; however, Gabby feels that the real reason for the new furniture is to erase her mother's lingering presence.

Thinking of Anna causes her to swing her trinity knot necklace back and forth on its chain. This nervous habit is a clue to anyone that she's thinking, and those thoughts right now are not happy ones. She needs to tell Brett that Stan will be convalescing here at the ranch.

Brett pulls her closer to him and squeezes her hand.

"You know I love you, Gabby." She looks up at him with wet eyes. "Hey, what's all this?" A tear rolls down her cheek.

So much has happened in a short period of time: her dad got married, she found out she was pregnant, she left for D.C., Brett proposed, she lost the baby, and now thinking of her mother, and the baby, and Stan, the waterworks flow.

"I'm so sorry. I'm a terrible person," she sobs. "I'm moody and bitchy—and I haven't been very nice to you lately. How can you possibly love me?"

He wipes her tears and kisses her forehead. "God, you're beautiful." He smiles and leans back and looks up to the sky.

"Okay, okay, I love you because you are drop-dead gorgeous. You're smart, and when you look at me and smile, I think I'm the luckiest man in the world. And when we kiss, it's like something I've never experienced before. I can't get enough of you. I don't know how else to describe it."

"Tell me more. I want to hear more." She sniffles.

"I love you because you're natural and wholesome. You appreciate nature. You love the ranch. We have that in common. You can be a city gal with the best of them but your heart is here." Before she can chime in, he continues. "This is where my heart is. Here out in God's country. Here with open space. I'm glad we share that." He pulls her in for a tighter hug. "How's that for an answer? Oh, oh...and let's not forget to mention the incredible sex."

She looks up and grins. "Oh, you just had to go there."

"I wish." He touches her cheek. "I've missed that. Do you think you're ready?"

She is saved from answering as her father's truck is making its way up the long drive from the road to the main house. The doctor had cleared her for all activities a week ago, including sex, but she hadn't made any attempt to share this information with Brett.

He stands and walks to the edge of the porch and waits for the couple to emerge from the vehicle. He shakes King's hand. "Welcome back, sir." He then reaches for Rita and assists her up the steps. "Any success?"

Rita's eyes light up. "Not only did we purchase new family room furniture but we also bought a new bedroom set. It's so pretty. I just love it. And that new family room furniture will make things so much easier for Stan."

Brett pulls his shoulders back and opens his mouth to speak. Rita has read the shock on his face and continues, "Yes, Stan is going to recover here. No one can take better care of him than his mother." She gives Gabby a wide-eyed stare. "He's coming tomorrow. I can hardly wait. I just hope the furniture will be delivered before he arrives. I want this place to be as cheery as possible for my boy."

Brett is speechless. He looks from Rita to King, and then finally to Gabby. He shakes his head and gives Gabby a "did you know this?" stare.

She turns her head and can feel the heat rising in her face. She wanted to tell him but she didn't know how. How do you tell the man who loves you that another man who has feelings for you is going to be living under the same roof? She knew Brett wouldn't take this news too kindly, and from the shocked look on his face, she was right. She lowers her head. Ella had shared with Gabby that Stan took his road trip to help him forget about her. She feels responsible for the accident, and now Brett is upset with her. Will Stan also hold her responsible? No wonder she is moody and cries. Life is so complicated.

"Oh, Stan's coming here...tomorrow?" Brett asks. "How long will he be here?"

"Depends," says Rita. "I told him he can stay as long as he likes." She wraps her arm around King's waist and reaches on her toes to give him a kiss. "Right, honey?"

King looks at Brett and even though he nods in agreement, his eyes tell a different story.

Seconds later, Jamie rings the bell signaling that dinner is ready.

"Let's eat," King says. "I'm starved." He ushers Rita into the ranch house.

Brett follows, holding the door for Gabby. "We need to talk," he whispers in a low voice.

It is customary for Gabby and Brett to take a walk after dinner, and tonight Brett is eager to get her alone to find out what she knows about Stan's visit. He pulls her in tight as soon as they are out of sight of others.

"Why do you love me?" he asks. Gabby stands back in surprise. This was not the question she anticipated.

"It's payback, your turn." From the hard tone of his voice, she can sense his anger.

"Why do I love you?" she repeats. She pauses briefly and then turns to face him. "I love you because you're so handsome—those green eyes and your dimple, not to mention the way your brown curls fall on the nape of your neck." She reaches up and twirls a brown curl around her finger.

"That's all physical, doesn't count." He lifts his eyebrows and his eyes are piercing. She can read his rage even in the dim light as the sun is close to the horizon. He isn't going to make this easy for her. She will need to give a better answer, add some humor to make him smile, then all will be forgiven.

She says teasingly, "It's the sex. It's incredible."

"Really." He pulls her in again. "I think I forgot. Ready to find out if it's still incredible?" He caresses her bottom.

"Brett, please." She pushes him away. "I'm sorry, but I'm just not ready yet."

"Of course, you're not ready yet. Stan's coming." His voice is sharp.

"You're mad."

"Of course I'm mad. Good old Stan. When were you going to tell me?"

"I wanted to tell you but the timing wasn't right. I knew that you would act like this."

"Don't put this on me," he yells.

"Keep your voice down. Rita will hear," she whispers.

He pulls her farther down the path away from the house. "I'm more upset about you not telling me, Gabby. It's a trust issue. You keeping things from me is not a good way to have a relationship." He stops walking and kicks the dirt with his boots.

"So you thought Brett doesn't need to know. Is that it, Gabby?" His stare is piercing. "You still have feelings for him? You're playing us against each other?" Then he says in a high-pitched voice as if mocking her. "Oh, Brett, tell me why you love me?" He places his hands on his hips and his eyes are wild. "Are you going to ask Stan the same question and compare answers? Is this some sick test?"

"Brett, stop it. You're acting like a jealous little boy." She reaches for his hand but he pulls it away.

"Jealous, damn straight, I have every right to be jealous. Stan loves you, Gabby. He asked you to marry him. I feel like such a fool."

"Stan felt obligated to ask. I was alone and pregnant."

"Is that what you tell yourself? Is that how you can sleep at night? It was your choice to be alone. You didn't tell me. You ran off. Do you know what you did to me? To us? You haven't learned one thing." He looks out into the distant horizon. "I'm a fool. I believed that you changed but you haven't changed a bit."

"Brett, don't be like this." She tugs on his arm. "Please, don't be like this." Her tears start flowing. "It's not that way. I love you."

"Love isn't keeping things from one another." He throws his hands up in the air and turns to walk toward the bunkhouse. Stopping and turning back to face her, he says, "I can't believe that Stan is coming here, to our ranch." He kicks the dirt and shakes his head.

"Where are you going? Look who's running now." She wipes her eyes on her sleeve.

"How does it feel? I'm going to bed, princess." He calls over his shoulder, "When you figure it out, let me know."

"Brett, you can't leave like this. We need to talk."

He turns to face her once again. "We should have talked a while ago. Enjoy Stan. I'm sure you have things to do to get ready for his arrival. I certainly don't want to keep you."

"Brett, stop. Come back."

She could run after him. She doesn't. *He'll be better in the morning. He needs time. He's right; I should have told him.* She bites her lip and pulls in a deep breath. She has made a mess of things. It won't be easy for her or Brett with Stan living here. Maybe she should go back to her condo in town, away from Stan and away from Brett. She still needs to grieve the loss of her child, not be a referee trying to keep two grown man apart. She doesn't need all this aggravation.

She turns to walk back to the house at a slow pace, wiping away more tears. The creeping of the rocking chair on the porch alerts her that she can't slip into the house unnoticed.

"He didn't take it well, did he?" A voice calls from the dark shadow. It is her daddy. She strains her eyes to see if he is alone. "I knew it would be a problem but I can't say no to Rita. Not on this matter. Stan needs help and he's family. Brett's a sensible man. He'll come around. He's in shock. Can't say I blame him." The rocker squeaks. "It would have been better for him to hear the news from you."

"Oh, Daddy, don't you go and defend him." She sniffles again.

King stands and moves to the glider. "Come here." He pats the seat next to him. Sitting down, she leans her head on his chest. "Things are not as bad as they seem. It's good that Brett's upset, means he loves you." The glider swings back and forth. "However, it's a shame he found out the way he did."

"I don't need a lecture. I feel bad enough. You're right, I should have been the one to tell him."

"You messed up, kitten." He squeezes her shoulder and the glider groans under their weight.

"He's hurt."

"He'll get over it. Let him sleep on it. I'll keep him busy tomorrow. He'll come around. Trust your old man." He peers down at her face and smiles. "Wipe those tears and let's be grateful that we still have a Stan to cause problems. His injuries were pretty serious from what I understand. It will all work out. Trust me."

That night, Gabby tosses and turns in her bed. Several times she picks up her phone to text Brett, but erases the message before sending. *Let him stew a bit*, she thinks. She told him he was being unreasonable, but is Brett right? It is true that Stan was there for her this spring when she was going through a rough time. There she was, pregnant with Richard's child, and lost as to what to do. At the time she had relied on Stan's strength and his wisdom.

Brett was right. She had never given him the chance to be there for her. Like today, she never told him, and she ran. He had to travel across the country and track her down. She drew in her lip.

Maybe Brett has a right to be concerned. The last time she saw Stan, it was on a star-filled evening just a month ago at Will and Ella's wedding. And, yes, Stan professed his love. Is she naïve to believe that she and Stan can be "just friends"? Is that why she found it hard to tell Brett about Stan coming to the ranch?

CHAPTER 11

Gabby paces back and forth, repeatedly glancing out the window toward the long drive that meets the main road. She has sequestered herself in her bedroom as she doesn't want anyone to misinterpret her anxiety by calling it something that it's not. She wrings her hands and then rubs her forehead as if coaxing her memory to the surface. It has been a little over a month since she last saw Stan. Sure, they spoke a few times on the phone but only small, superficial conversations. Is Brett right to be jealous of Stan recovering at the ranch? Does she still have feelings for him? No, she doesn't love Stan, so why is she so nervous?

She pulls her phone from her pocket to check the time. Rita estimated their arrival thirty minutes ago. What is taking so long? Gabby has had plenty of time to think this afternoon. She had wished to make up with Brett so that when Stan arrived in Texas he would find them to be a strong, united couple.

Yesterday she sent Brett a text in an attempt to dissolve their disagreement, but he had replied, "Sorry, can't talk now. Catch you later." She guesses that later has yet to come as she is still waiting for a reply. At breakfast this morning her daddy shared that Brett was in Fort Worth helping Rusty to trailer some cattle for market and that he would be gone for a few days. So today, she will face Stan alone.

Her thoughts are interrupted by the mellow hum of an engine approaching, and she leans on the window sill, pressing her nose against the pane. A van is making its way up the drive, kicking up dust that leaves a dirt cloud hovering behind. *It's them...show time. Pull yourself together.* She straightens her skirt and checks her profile in the mirror one last time.

When she exits the screen door on the front porch, she finds her daddy opening the side door of the van while the driver is getting a wheelchair out the back. Listening to Rita's excited chatter causes Gabby's pulse to race a little faster. *Put on your happy face. You've rehearsed this meeting at least a hundred times. Stop acting like a schoolgirl.*

Her daddy nods his head toward the middle section of the van and then rolls his eyes. Gabby guesses the trip from the airport was challenging.

"Let me come out first so I can help," Rita yells, pushing King away from the door.

"Okay, dear, I was just trying to give a hand." King backs up another step.

After exiting, Rita shouts back over her shoulder. "Stan, there's a big step to the ground. You let Wayne guide you, all right, sweetheart?"

Stan lowers his head and, before he leans on the seat to assist him to stand, his eyes meet Gabby's. Neither speaks. Neither moves.

"Stan, you need help?" asks Rita.

Not taking his eyes off Gabby, Stan smiles, so she forces a smile in return. Then his eyes dip to her waist, and she lowers her eyes and bites her lip. Memories flood—thoughts of Stan feeling her baby kick, offering to take birthing classes, their last evening before she came home to Texas, and then the tragic loss of her baby. Her breathing quickens and her world starts spinning. *Take a deep breath, steady, I can do this.* She twirls her trinity knot back on forth on its chain.

"Gabby." She looks up to see concern on Stan's face.

"Hello, Stan. It's good to see you." She takes a deep breath.

"I've been worried about you." He pushes himself to a standing position and steps to the edge of the van. He uses his arm to swing his cast in the same direction.

Her eyes grow wide and follow his blue casts, one on his arm and the other on his leg.

"I know, it looks massive—heavy too." He smiles at her again.

Rita places her hands on her hips. "Stan, let Wayne help you. It's hot standing here. You'll be much cooler in the house. Let's get you inside."

Stan hands Gabby his crutch and holds onto King for support as he slides cautiously out of the van. His next challenge is to maneuver the three steps up to the porch. With King supporting him under his shoulder, Stan grips the railing and propels himself up the stairs and into the wheelchair. He wipes his brow and exhales. "That was harder than I anticipated."

"Not to worry, I'm having a carpenter come and build a ramp since you'll be here for a while. In time, you'll be able to come and go as you please," King says.

"Thanks, sir. That's kind of you."

"That's the least we can do for you," Rita says. "You let us know, anything you need and we'll make sure you get it. Come, come inside. Gabby, get the door for us." She turns Stan's wheelchair to face the door.

"Yes, ma'am." Gabby opens the door. She finds it easier to smile at Stan now that they both share common ground as each was caught in an embarrassing moment. Having Stan around will be interesting.

Later that evening, dinner conversation started with a light, jovial air. Several times, though, Gabby has felt Stan's stare but she pretended not to notice and tried to avoid glancing in his direction. Why was he challenging her?

Still, she's found herself smiling during the meal as she watched Rita hovering over her son, cutting his meat and buttering his dinner roll. The atmosphere changes when Jamie directs a question to him.

"Stan, tell us about your accident." A hush falls over the room and Stan's eyes go from Jamie to his mother.

"You don't want to hear about that." He shakes his head, taking a sip of water.

"I think it's a great question, Jamie." Rita puts her hands on her hips and stares at him. "I would also like to know how you managed to wind up in that chair with those broken and smashed bones."

He looks from Rita to King, as if he is looking for King to save him, but King remains silent.

Stan clears his throat. "Well, since all of you seem to want to know all the details of how this went down." He looks around the table again and his eyes rest on Gabby; this time she does not look away. He takes a sip of water and begins. "It was a beautiful, sunny day, the perfect weekend for a joy ride on a motorcycle. I was headed south to the Dragon's Tail. I've heard that it's the most traveled sport road in the country."

Gabby sees how his eyes light up when he speaks of the beautiful mountain scenery and about how he enjoys riding. When it comes to describing the accident, she is sure that he's intentionally omitting some of the specific, graphic details so as not to upset his mother. He seems to skim over the event as if he's telling about rain in a weather forecast instead of a crash that nearly left him for dead. However, when he speaks of a future ride to finish the trek he started, Rita stands and abruptly pushes her chair from the table.

"I've heard enough of this foolish talk." Then she starts to clear the table and says to Gabby, "Wheel Stan outside on the porch. I'll make some coffee and bring out dessert." Staring at Stan, Rita says in a forceful tone, "I want him to catch the sunset his first evening here and for him to be damn grateful that he is *alive* to see another sunset. Silly talk about getting back on that damn bike. Crazy!" She presses her hand hard into his shoulder.

Stan maintains his grin. "Mom, I am grateful." Then he reaches up and pats his mother's hand.

"Sure thing, let's go." Gabby stands and takes the handles of Stan's wheelchair and being mindful of his casted leg, spins the chair away from the table in a wide turn.

Once out on the porch she says to him, "You okay?"

"I'm good. It's good to be here again. It's good to be here with you. I've missed you."

She blushes and turns away in hopes that he doesn't see.

"Where's your fiancé? Is that his title even though I don't see a ring on your finger?" He reaches up and grabs her hand.

"Brett's working. He's in Fort Worth with Rusty. They took some cattle to market. And...we've been busy." She makes an attempt to pull her hand away but Stan holds on more tightly. "He'll be back tomorrow."

"It's no secret I don't like the guy. With him away, I have you all to myself." He brings her hand up to his lips for a kiss.

She jumps back fast and this time she is able to pull her hand away.

"I've missed you." His stare cuts through her, making her feel ashamed.

"Please don't." She reads sincerity on his face and turns away. She does suffer guilt for leading him on earlier this summer. At one time, she did consider a relationship with him, but she explained all of that. Besides, she has enough to deal with these days. Bringing up the past won't change anything.

"I'm sorry about the baby. I can't even imagine what you have been through. I would have been here for you. You know that, right?"

His pleading words mixed with his emotional tone are more than she can bear. She closes her eyes and is unable to stop a tear from splashing down her cheek.

"I care about you." He wipes her face with his hand. "I still love you."

Those words cause her breathing to quicken and her throat to tighten. She gazes off into the horizon. Together they are quiet, watching as the sun slowly slips away and the shadows lengthen.

The hues of pink, peach and violet fill the sky and they start to hear the crickets.

She is first to speak, in a voice that is just a little louder than a whisper. "His name was Jacob."
She allows him to hold her hand and his warm touch is comforting. She continues searching the horizon and touches her now flat stomach. "He was beautiful. I'll never forget him."

Stan gazes up at her from his wheelchair. "He was lucky to have you as a mother."

"You think?" She pinches her lip and another tear leaves a track down her face.

"I don't think, I know." He clasps her hand tighter.

She looks down and finds his earnest face. His expression matches his words. The release of the painful memory envelops her and she is unable to control her sobs. He pulls her down into his lap. "Come here. I'm so sorry...so terribly sorry."

She leans her head into Stan's chest. She feels his warmth and his strength. She has painted a happy face for many days, but here with Stan, her defenses are shattered. A moist drop falls on her forehead and she knows that he shares in her sorrow.

"I'm so sorry." Pulling away from him, Gabby wipes her tears on her hands. "Here you are comforting me and you almost died. And... I'm probably hurting you." She gives a little chuckle as she stands, being careful to avoid his injured arm and leg.

"I don't mind." There's a twinkle in his eye.

Before she can respond, Rita comes through the screen door carrying a tray of cookies, followed by King, who has a tray with a carafe of coffee and mugs.

"Damn, we missed the sunset, Wayne," Rita says.

Stan pipes in quickly with a cheerful tone, "It just went down a few minutes ago."

Gabby stands at the far edge of the porch, where she moved upon hearing the door open, in an effort to compose herself. Embarrassed that she has cried in front of Stan, she rubs her forehead. Why did she accept his comfort? He's in a wheelchair, and it would appear to anyone around that she must have initiated their exchange of physical contact. She had no business sitting in his lap. It bothers her that she is weak and vulnerable. There is no need to cause Rita or her daddy worry. They'll have their hands full taking care of Stan. *I wish Brett were here. I need him.*

This night is not going as she had planned. She had rehearsed her lines as if performing in a play. She had practiced faking a smile. Why is she so pathetic? She wanted Stan to see her happy—to see that she had made the right choice when she chose Brett. Instead, she broke down. Will Stan read more into her tears than grieving the loss of her baby? By allowing herself to find comfort in his arms, has she led him to believe that she has feelings for him? Maybe it's good that Brett isn't back from Fort Worth, back to see her tears, back to see her in Stan's arms.

Interrupting her thoughts, Rita asks, "Gabby, are you having dessert with us?"

She turns. "Sorry, I was just thinking about Brett. I need to call him. I must have left my phone upstairs. Go ahead. I'll be back in a flash." She dashes past them and hurries up the staircase.

In her bedroom, she picks up her cell and dials Brett's number.

The call goes straight to voicemail. She leaves a message: *Sorry to miss you. Call me back. I love you.*

There, she's said it. Those three little words packed with big meaning. Did she say it to convince herself of her feelings? Armed with her phone, she glances into the mirror, wipes a smear of mascara from under her eyes and straightens her long blond strands. She double-checks one last time to be sure all traces of her tears are erased before she skips down the stairs to join the others on the porch.

After dessert and coffee, everyone is quiet. Stan says, "It's been a long day. I'm going to hit the sack." He taps his blue cast. "It will be interesting to see how I manage getting in and out of the bathroom with this big guy."

Earlier that week, Rita turned King's office into a makeshift bedroom. The only enclosed room on the first floor, it is small and the full-size bed takes up most of the space, but it does have a bathroom complete with a shower. Still the bathroom is too small for a wheelchair to enter, but it is the best they can do to accommodate Stan.

"Let me help you," Rita says. "Anything you need, you let me know."

"Yes, Mother. But somehow I'm sure that you thought of everything." Rita wheels him around and King holds the door for them.

"Good night, y'all," Stan calls over his shoulder while sporting a big smile.

Gabby giggles. "I see you're still working on that Texas twang and the lingo."

"Glad you noticed."

"Good night, Stan," says King and he kisses Rita on the cheek. "Call me if you need help."

CHAPTER 12

King sits on a rocking chair and motions for Gabby to take the chair next to him. "Stan seems to need help getting around. I'll get that ramp built as soon as possible. It'll do him good to get outside a bit." He stops rocking and looks over at her. "How do you think tonight went?"

"Fine—yes, it went pretty well. I hope it goes this smoothly when Brett returns." She leans back in her chair. "I tried calling Brett but he didn't pick up. Have you heard from either him or Rusty?"

"I didn't speak with Brett. However, I did speak with my foreman. Rusty says he got a good price for the cattle."

"I know that makes you happy." She stares out into the night sky, taking in all the stars.

"Sure does. Rusty and Brett won't be home until late tomorrow evening. Seems like there are some cowboys up there who are practicing for the rodeo. Those guys were bragging at the bar so Rusty and Brett got themselves an invitation to check 'em out. Rusty'll time them." King chuckles. "They have no idea who Brett is. I'm sure if they did, they would be more cautious."

"Sounds important," Gabby says.

"Everyone here has high hopes that Brett will make it to the state championship. Last rodeo, he won by almost a full second. That's huge in the rodeo world. Rusty knows one of the cowboys as he took the state title last year in the steer tie-down competition. It'll be worth it for them to take a look since they're already there."

Then, in a serious voice that gets her attention, he says, "Brett needs to buckle down, practice every day. I can't have him distracted."

"And you're looking at me?" She places her hand over her heart.

"I didn't mention any names. I made a statement." He sits forward in his chair. "Brett doesn't need any distractions. He needs to focus."

"Having Stan here is a big distraction, not me, Daddy."

"So true, darlin'. I agree with you but what was I to do? Rita here is all upset. I can't tell her no. I'd be viewed as a monster." He scrunches up his face and sticks out his tongue.

Gabby giggles. "Seriously, with everyone counting on Brett, I know he feels the pressure. He doesn't want to disappoint anyone, especially you. However, Stan and Brett in the same room..." She shakes her head.

"It's like oil and vinegar. I know, I know." He takes a sip of his coffee. "I saw him watching you. It's obvious that he still has feelings for you. If I can see it, Brett will pick up on it. That's one of the reasons I sent him to market with Rusty. I wanted to assess the situation myself. I foolishly thought that after all this time, the motorcycle accident and his flirt with death...I had hopes that Stan would have moved on."

King rocks back and forth before adding, "It's good that Stan has two casts. That should keep Brett from decking him, at least for a few days." He chuckles again.

"Brett wouldn't hit Stan."

"Now look who's defending Mr. Brett. I'm pretty sure if Brett saw what I did tonight, you all cuddled up on Stan's lap, Stan would be wearing a black eye, probably worse."

She stares ahead. "It wasn't what you think." Her daddy and Rita must have witnessed their exchange. *Damn.*

"Doesn't matter what I think. What matters is what Brett will think. Just sayin', I don't want my golden boy to forget that he can be a star." Before she has an opportunity to respond, King says, "I ran into old man Lohman today. He's so envious that Brett is working for me. Remember, Brett grew up over on that ranch, and his old man worked all of his life for Lohman. Jacob Matthews was a fine man and he was good at trainin' young guys, teachin' 'em how to herd the cattle."

Gabby wasn't sure her attention was needed as King seemed to be caught up in reminiscing, but she is on the edge of her seat after hearing Jacob Matthews' name mentioned. Brett rarely spoke of his family, and she had never thought to ask her daddy. Now that her buried son shares this man's name, she listens intently.

"Jacob would take these young boys to train. Many of them grew up on the ranch, just like your guy, Brett. It was the only way of life they knew. They grew up riding practically before they could even run straight. That's where Jacob would come in. He would watch these guys and know exactly what to tweak so they could be just a few milliseconds more efficient. Efficiency, that's the key, Gabby, one of the keys to becoming a star. That's what Jacob Matthews did for Stewart."

He hesitates and glances at her. "You're probably too young to remember Stewart. He was the longest running tie-down champion in the state, and no one has come close to his record. He was a joy to watch. Sure, he had some natural ability, but under Jacob's guidance, that boy was the best." King takes a deep breath and proceeds with his tale.

"Your guy, Brett, reminds me of Stewart. Rides like him. If I took video of Stewart and Brett and put them side by side, you wouldn't be able to tell them apart. Too bad, there was no video back when Jacob was riding, but if my memory serves me well, I would say that Brett rides just like his old man. But Brett needs some practice since he was away from it, off being a tennis pro."

He shakes his head. "Can't understand who gives up the rodeo for tennis but what do I know, right? I'm praying for muscle memory. Since old man Jacob isn't around anymore, I keep prayin' that he'll visit from heaven and whisper into Brett's ear. Some people call that intuition. I on the other hand call it divine intervention."

Gabby leans forward on her rocker. "Tell me more about Jacob. What was he like?"

"Old man Jacob was a real Western ranch hand. He was dependable and, like I said, the best at what he did. He would go out and drink with the guys but he could hold his liquor. Can't say I ever recall him being rowdy or unruly."

"What did he look like?"

"He was tall, but a lean man. No extra fat anywhere on that guy. Could be because his wife died soon after they were married.

Without a woman cookin' that Southern fried food, a man is less likely to be heavy. Jacob was lean but he wasn't mean. He had the patience of Job. After losing his wife, he never remarried. His job was ranching, grooming champions for the tour, and raising Brett. He was a good man, kitten."

He reaches over and pats her hand. "Brett comes from good stock, Gabby. He's a fine man. I don't know what's all going on in that pretty little head of yours. I know that you're still grieving and confused. I understand that Stan was there for you when you were making some difficult life decisions, but don't confuse kindness and empathy for love. You feel bad for Stan, and he has a long way to go before he fully recovers. I get it. You hurt for him."

She is speechless. She leans back against the wooden chair and rocks. King squeezes her hand. "Brett can do this. Rusty knows it and I know it. The only person who doesn't believe it is Brett. Any help you can give that boy would be greatly appreciated." He winks.

Just then a voice from within the house yells, "Wayne, honey, we need you."

"Guess I've been summoned." He smiles, stands and gives her a kiss on the cheek. "Make up with Brett."

Later that night, unable to sleep, Gabby stares at the ceiling. There was a missed call on her phone when she got back inside after speaking with her daddy. *At least he's not avoiding me.* She keeps going over the conversations she had with both Stan and her daddy. She had never intended to mislead Stan, giving him hopes that he still has a chance to win her love. Maybe her ever-so-wise daddy is right. Maybe she is confused, mistaking her feelings of empathy for love. She knows that she loves Brett, but maybe she's having doubts because she and Stan shared some precious memories. She was clinging to those, as memories were the only thing that she had to draw her closer to her child—and the man in those memories is Stan, not Brett.

She touches her fingers on her left hand and is reminded of the absence of an engagement ring. Surely, if she and Brett were serious about their commitment, shouldn't they have made some plans? Bought a ring? Set a date? Anything to make their engagement official? Earlier Stan had commented on the obvious.

Suddenly her thoughts turn to the architectural plans for their house on the edge of the ranch property by the lake. She remembers how excited she had been to see the ropes and stakes marking the foundation and how she'd anticipated sharing this surprise with Brett. She'd shown him the plans and then asked him to marry her. All of this seems like a lifetime ago. Losing Jacob is all she has thought about in weeks. It's time for her to move forward. Creating a future with Brett will help. She closes her eyes and paints a picture—a tall, suntanned body, with that brown wavy hair, emerald green eyes and a dimple. He is handsome and he is her man.

Her phone vibrates and Brett's face appears on the screen. She smiles and answers in a sexy, low voice.

"Did I wake you up?" he asks. "It's late, I shouldn't have called."

"No, I was awake. I don't want to bother Daddy and Rita. I'm glad you called. I was just thinking about you and about us. I've missed you. When are you coming back?"

"Not until tomorrow, late evening. Rusty and I met these guys.

One of them was the state champion last year. Well, we're going to an arena just a few miles north of here to watch them practice."

He clears his throat. "Sorry I missed your call. We were at the bar listening to these guys brag on and on. It will be good to see if they're as good as they say they are. The one guy may be the reigning champion but, really, he's such a bragger."

Remembering her daddy's request, she says, "You're as good as any of them. I know it."

"Well, thanks for the vote of confidence but...I don't know about that."

"Yes, you're just as good, even better. Believe in yourself." There, she has given Brett a pep talk. Her daddy would be proud.

"How's it going with Stan?" His question returns her thoughts to their conversation.

"Okay, but he's not very mobile. He needs help getting in and out of the wheelchair. At least until he gets the cast off his arm in another two weeks."

"I'll sleep better knowing that he isn't sneaking up the stairs into your room at night."

She giggles. "You have nothing to worry about. I love you, silly."

"I don't trust him, Gabby."

"When you get here you'll see that he is harmless. Really, Brett, he's my stepbrother." *Wow, have I just said that? Let's change the subject.* "I miss you."

"Tell me more about that?" She can hear flirting in his tone.

"I'm not going to have phone sex with you."

"No, well, darn, I wanted Rusty to have a wet dream."

"Brett, is Rusty listening?"

85

"No, Rusty is asleep and snoring. I can't sleep with that racket."

She laughs. "Poor, poor, baby. Hey, I was thinking...thinking about us. We should have an engagement party. Do something to make our engagement official. Have some fun. Make some memories."

"You know I don't care much for parties, but if this is what it will take to make you happy, I'm all for it. Just let me know when and where and I'll be there."

"You look so handsome in a tux. I'm the one who should be worried. Those single gals will have their hands all over you. I will have to beat them away with a whip."

"See who started the phone sex. Tell me more about your whip."

"Stop it, Brett. Be serious and don't let Rusty hear you. How embarrassing it will be for both of us when he talks to Daddy."

"Seriously, Gabby, I'm fine with a party. Like I said, whatever you want, princess. I just want things to go back to the way they were. And I want everyone to know that you're mine."

"Would that include Stan?"

"Especially Stan." He laughs. "Plan your party."

"It's our party," she reminds him.

"Yes, our party. Morning will be here fast. I need to put in these earplugs and try to get some sleep. Love you."

"Love you too. Good night."

CHAPTER 13

Waking up the next morning, Gabby realizes that sleep came easily that night after her phone call with Brett. She is glad that things between them seem to be back to normal. It's a reminder that sometimes time and distance are all a situation needs. Now, it is as if they never had a disagreement, and with their relationship back on track, she wants to keep it that way. She makes a mental note to be more cautious around Stan, as Brett would not take kindly to witnessing a scene like her daddy saw last night on the porch.

Still in her nightgown, she sits at her desk and flips through her calendar in search of a date for their engagement party. There isn't enough time to plan a party in September. Flipping through the months on the calendar, she sees a large red circle around the first Friday in October. This date is her opening reception at The Gallery in Austin. She has waited two years to be a solo artist showcased at this venue. Rechecking the calendar, it would be hard to organize another party that month and she really doesn't want to wait until

November. It will be best for her and Brett to have a celebration soon because it will help both of them to put the tragic past behind.

October is such a beautiful time of year in Texas, with the weather still warm but not too warm, and the evenings are delightful. Since she has to plan and finance the opening night reception, why not turn that night into an engagement party? All of her friends and family will be there, and if she keeps the venue open to the public, The Gallery should be happy for the publicity. She already has half of the planning done: the venue, the caterer, and the invite list. Yes, it will be the perfect night. All she needs to do to turn the art reception into an engagement party is to make a special e-vite, buy a knockout dress, call the florist, and ask the caterer to add additional items to the menu. It will be so simple.

She rummages through her desk to find a pad of paper and a pen. In bold letters at the top of the page she writes ENGAGEMENT PARTY. She starts her list and then, biting on the end of the pen, she adds to it: a tux for Brett and champagne. Thinking of the bubbly makes the corners of her mouth turn up. She will ask her daddy to make the toast. She rubs her left hand, realizing that something is missing; Brett has never mentioned giving her an engagement ring. With some hesitation she adds a line to her list: shop for a ring.

As she opens the desk drawer to return the pen, she sees a photo. Holding it, she leans back in her chair. It was the selfie that Brett insisted they take in April right before King and Rita's wedding ceremony. In the picture, a handsome couple smiles back at her. That was only four months ago; however, the couple in the photo didn't have a clue as to all the challenges that their relationship would face in those future months. *Ignorance sure is bliss.* But even with all of the challenges that were handed to them, they are still a couple; they survived.

She wedges the photo into the corner of her vanity mirror. She will replace this snapshot with one showing a smiling, happy couple on the night of their engagement party. The party will give them a new start.

It is late morning when Gabby skips down the stairs. The dining room table is cleared of any evidence of breakfast, and Rita is at her computer while Stan sits in his wheelchair reading his iPad.

Rita peers over the rims of her glasses. "Well, look who has finally decided to join us. Even for you, this is late."

"Sorry, I was busy working." Both Stan and Rita stare at her.

"I've been working on my art exhibit for the show at The Gallery downtown next month. I'll need some of my pieces from ArtSmart, if that's okay."

"You can trade. Just don't leave me with empty walls. At this late date, I don't know who I could get to fill in for you," Rita says with concern.

"Oh, Mother," Stan says, "that would not be a problem. You can hang some of your own art."

"Yes, that's a great idea, Stan. Rita, you have only hung one or two of your pieces since I've been working there. Stan's right. You should take an entire wall."

Stan is beaming.

"I don't know," says Rita. "My work isn't that good."

"Yes, it is. You have a unique style. It's different and I think folks like different." Gabby stands with her hands on her hips. "It's time, Rita. You started this gallery so you could display your art."

Rita shakes her head. "But I have bills to pay."

"Mother, you're too critical. Your art is great. Put it on the walls."

"Think about it, Rita." Gabby goes over and hugs her. "When you're ready to hang, I can help. It'll be fun."

"I'll think about it."

"And I'll supervise." Stan has his good arm reaching out toward Gabby. "Hey, where's my good morning hug?" When she hesitates, he adds, "I need some of that."

Reluctantly, she leans into Stan and embraces him. Pulling her in tight, he whispers in her ear, "You smell great," and then nuzzles her ear.

She pulls away as fast as she can and feels the heat creeping into her face. He has managed to turn this innocent good morning hug into something sexual. He's making her feel guilty as if she is cheating on Brett. If Brett saw this, his blood would boil.

Let this be a warning. Stan's past behavior is a good indicator of his behavior in the future. He doesn't deserve to be given the benefit of the doubt. I need to stay far away from him. Maybe having words with Stan in Rita's presence will keep him at bay.

"Stan, please don't do that. It makes me uncomfortable when you hold so tight and whisper in my ear."

"I haven't done anything wrong." He lifts his hands up in the air as if he is totally innocent. "What's wrong with giving a good morning hug?"

Rita looks at them with a furrowed brow and shakes her head as if in disapproval. Gabby hopes that she understands and places the blame on Stan where it belongs.

Rita changes the subject. "Jamie has already cleared away breakfast and she's preparing lunch to take out to the boys working in the fields. So, you'll have to help yourself...and, Gabby, I'm glad you're back working. I really could use your help at ArtSmart. The gallery has been limping along since you left in April. I hired a part-time gal but she is tired of working weekends. Can I schedule you this weekend?"

"I know that I owe you some time. You have been very understanding."

"Then I'll take that answer as a yes. I'll text Rachel right now. She will be thrilled to have both Friday and Saturday off." She turns back to face the computer.

"Does that mean I'm working Friday and Saturday—day and evening?" Gabby tilts her head to the side.

Rita turns her chair back to face Gabby and she leans forward with her hands on her thighs. "You are behind on your weekend shifts and I need to stay here with Stan. Since we close early on Saturday, it would be foolish for someone to cover a few hours in the afternoon. It would really help. Rachel has been a doll in all of the months that you have been away. It's the least..." Gabby's mouth had opened wide to protest but she manages to button her lip. "You can do," Rita finishes.

Gabby hopes that when Brett follows her into town and isn't here to practice, her daddy will see that it is Rita's doing, as she dictates the schedule. If Gabby is in town at the gallery, of course, Brett will want to spend the weekend with her. This is not going to be her battle. She'll allow her daddy to handle Rita. Gabby is sure that this will be her only full weekend working until after the rodeo.

"Sure, Rita, if you need me." She fakes a smile.

On second thought, she realizes working will get her away from Stan. Rita's a pretty smart gal, and from all the exchanges she has seen and hearing Gabby's own warning to Stan, maybe arranging for Gabby to get away from the ranch is a tactful way to diffuse the situation. Rita is probably trying to be helpful.

On her way to the kitchen, Gabby calls over her shoulder, "You are planning to attend my art reception in October—at The Gallery, right?"

"Yes, dear," Rita says. "It's right here on my calendar, the first Friday in October. I'm so happy you're working again. It's a good thing."

Good, Rita has plans to attend so I'll tell her about the reception turning into our engagement party after I speak with Brett. Gabby raises her eyebrows, pleased that her plan is coming together.

CHAPTER 14

After speaking briefly to Jamie, Gabby grabs a few apples from the bowl in the kitchen and shoves them in her jacket pockets. She wonders why neither Stan nor Rita commented on her attire. She's going riding and the apples will be a welcomed treat for the horses. Lady, her brown mare, always expects a treat and Gabby doesn't wish to disappoint. She's missed being in the saddle and today seems to be the perfect day for a ride. Setting the date for the engagement party and focusing more on her relationship with Brett reminds her that she has not been out to the land where she and Brett have plans to build a house.

She takes in a deep breath as she looks around the magnificent countryside. The air is clear and there is a warm breeze from the west. That dark cloud of grief that has hovered over her for weeks seems to have dissipated. She doesn't understand the reason for her happiness—maybe it's due to making up with Brett or the chance to plan a party or possibly the combination of both. Whatever it is, she is grateful to be feeling close to normal again.

Feeling hungry, she reaches into her pocket for an apple and takes a big juicy bite. As she wipes the wetness from her chin, she rounds the turn, surprised to see a red Ferrari parked near the barn. A Ferrari is a rare sight and to have one here on the ranch could only mean one thing. *Oh my God, someone should have warned me that Richard was here. First I had to deal with Stan and now Richard...and all in the same morning. Lord, help me.* She rolls her eyes and starts to reminisce about the years she and Richard were dating.

It was soon after Richard came to town that her daddy introduced them. They were an item for two years and everyone assumed that they would marry, until she ended their relationship just this February. Then, she started dating Brett and felt like she was floating on air. Her world turned upside down two months later, when she discovered that she was pregnant, and Richard was the father. Now, Gabby hangs her head and has a heavy feeling in her gut. She never told Richard about his son.

Richard is a lawyer and her daddy is among the oil and cattle ranchers backing him in his run for senator. Even though Richard is an outstanding attorney and he'll probably be a good politician, he wasn't a great boyfriend. After Gabby caught Richard cheating for the second time, she kicked him out the door. Initially upon hearing of the broken relationship, her father had pulled her to the side and asked her to consider reconciling with Richard, as King was sure that Richard would advance in the political scene and King had dreams of his little girl living in the governor's mansion. But she declined.

However, King himself had changed his tune before long. Shortly after Gabby started dating Brett, she noticed that King and Brett seemed to act like father and son. They shared many interests and her daddy mentioned that he was glad that there was a capable person to help her manage the ranch when he was gone. After that, there was no more mention of Richard. All in all, she knows her daddy meant well and just wants her to be happy.

Since their breakup, Richard has made some pretty offensive remarks about her. The few times their paths crossed in the last six months, it hasn't been pleasant. She believes his behavior demonstrates his way of controlling a situation that has left him wounded.

Stumbling over an uneven area of the gravel road, she is brought back to the present situation. She surmises Richard's visit to the ranch must be about the campaign. King is a huge financial backer and there is a lot at stake in this election, as several bills are in committee that can affect the oil business. Even though she and Richard are no longer a couple, because of the oil wells on the King property and her daddy's influence Richard will still be in her life.

She bites her lip and throws her shoulders back. *I'm not going to let Richard ruin my day. It doesn't matter that I never told him about Jacob. It doesn't matter anymore. It's better this way. Be polite. Besides, Richard will put on his best behavior in front of Daddy.*

With a brisk step, she walks down the gravel road, thinking that speeding up her gait will help overcome her urge to turn back. Rounding the corner, she comes to an abrupt halt. In her path stands a brunette dressed in a tight skirt and spike heels, her eyes glued to her cell phone. The crunch of the gravel with Gabby's abrupt stop causes her to look up.

Gabby gasps and places her hand on her chest. "Sorry, you scared me."

"I'm waiting for Richard." The woman gives Gabby the once-over look, smiles, and extends her hand. "Hi, I'm Amanda."

"Hello, I'm Gabby, Wayne King's daughter."

"Oh, yes, Richard has mentioned you. It's good to meet you."

Amanda's handshake is weak. Gabby doesn't think her hands were ever that smooth. *I wonder what she does for a living.*

Amanda starts to wave her hand like a fan. "I wish Richard would hurry. I don't want to ruin my heels in this dirt and I'm starting to sweat in this sun."

"I'll go and see what's keeping him," Gabby says.

"Would you, dear? That would help. I'm beginning to melt."

"Gladly." Gabby smiles back and tips her cowboy hat. Darn, she should have put on some blush or some mascara. *I must look like a tomboy.* Melt, did she say melt? Didn't the Wicked Witch of the West in "The Wizard of Oz" melt? Grinning, Gabby brushes a few strands of hair away from her face. Richard's choice in women always leaves her amazed. *What did he ever see in me? Did he date me just to get close to my daddy?*

When she enters the barn, it takes a few seconds for her eyes to adjust to the dim light. Loud voices are coming from the small makeshift office, and she is certain that her daddy and Richard are having a disagreement. Suddenly, a horse neighs and she knocks on his gate stall as she gives the half-eaten apple to him. The distraction works as the angry voices stop.

Richard pokes his head out from around the door frame of the office. "Well, Gabriella. It's so nice to see you." She ignores him and looks to her daddy and then her gaze returns to Richard. Still she doesn't acknowledge his greeting.

"Sorry if I interrupted but there's this gal out there who says that she's 'melting.'" Gabby lifts her hands and makes quotation marks with her fingers. "She certainly isn't dressed for the ranch, but then I see neither are you." She nods in Richard's direction and her eyes begin at his face and work their way down to his shoes.

He is in a full black suit, complete with a white dress shirt and navy blue tie, and he is wearing what appears to have been shiny black leather shoes but now they are covered in dust. He follows her eyes down to them, frowns and shakes his head. She lifts her eyebrows, smiles and crosses her arms in front of her chest.

King stands from behind the desk. "I think we're finished here."

Richard glances at his Rolex. "I do need to get back to town. I'll call you later."

"No need," King replies and gathers the papers in front of him and places them back into a folder and hands it to Richard. "I've given you my answer. You know what you need to do."

Moving over beside Gabby, King puts his arm around her waist. "So, to what do I owe this pleasure?"

Richard tries again. "I really hope that you will reconsider."

"Not happening. Your fancy gal is melting. It's best not to disappoint everyone today."

Richard throws his hands up in the air before turning around to leave. Gabby shrugs her shoulders and both she and King watch a defeated Richard walk away. Seconds later, they hear the Ferrari rev up, leaving a dust cloud in the air.

"Poor Richard," she says, shaking her head, her voice dripping sarcasm.

"Poor Richard. Lazy Richard is more his title. He wants it but

97

he doesn't want to do what needs to be done to get it. He wants me to hand him everything. Richard needs to stand tall and be tough. I know he can do it as I have watched that boy in the courtroom. He needs to work these men the same way he works the jurors." King shakes his head. "He'll handle it. If not, maybe it's best that he doesn't win this election. We need someone who will represent us, and if Richard isn't that guy then he isn't of any use."

King reaches up to turn off the light over the desk. "So, from the looks of it, you must be going out riding."

"Yes, I want to go out to the site of the house before I give the final okay to the contractor. He has left several messages last week and I haven't called him back. He says that if the foundation is dug in the next few weeks, the house could be finished by the end of the year."

King smiles. "That's my girl. It's good to have you back." He gives her a hug. "Let me help you saddle Lady. She sure has missed you."

"Thanks, Daddy. Do you want to join me?"

"Oh, kitten, I wish I could but I have to supervise the men. With Rusty gone, they tend to slack off but I'm waiting for Jamie to finish preparing their lunch and then I'll start out."

After saddling up Lady, he looks at his daughter with concern. "You sure you're up to this?"

Before answering, she pulls out one of the apples from her pocket and offers it to Lady and then gives the mare a pat.

"The doctor cleared me for all activities." She places her foot into the stirrup and swings her leg over the mare's back.

"You got your cell?" King lifts his hand to help shield his eyes from the sun. "Coverage is better lately. They added that new cell tower."

"Yes, sir, I've got the phone right here."

"If you need anything—"

She doesn't let him finish. "Yes, daddy. I'll be fine. Really, you worry too much."

"Kitten, I invited Brett to supper. He and Rusty should be back earlier than they first thought." He tips his hat. "Just thought you should know."

"That's fine. Not to worry, we've made up." She smiles as she pulls the reins, turning Lady around.

"Good, happy to hear that. Brett and Stan need to learn to play nice, so tonight is as good a night as any. I hope they can be civil to each other. One more thing, honey—I need Brett to focus on the rodeo. Okay, no distractions."

"Yes, Daddy, anything I can do to help."

"Darlin', keep Stan at a distance." King winks as he slaps Lady on the rump with his hat.

The mare trots down the gravel path and quickly Gabby urges her into a canter. Turning around one last time, she sees King watching. She knows he'll worry until she returns. She gives a slight wave before instructing Lady into a full gallop, forgetting the doctor's orders.

At first, she loves feeling the summer breeze on her face as they follow the path to the creek. The locusts are singing in harmony with the cardinals. A few falcons and a hawk grace the sky. *God, I have missed this.* Still, it doesn't take long until she is short of breath and has to slow down to a trot, while wiping the sweat from her brow.

Spending so much time in the house recovering from her miscarriage, her body is not acclimated to the intense Texas heat.

Along the trail before her, the terrain features a row of cedar trees and some prickly pear cactus, on cracked ground that cries out for much-needed rain. She realizes her own throat is parched. Damn, her unexpected visit with Richard caused her to forget to fill her water bottle. Why does she let him rattle her so?

Temperatures will be cooler in the shade of the oaks by the creek that runs right in front of the field, the future site of the house she and Brett will build. Thinking about the house puts a smile on her face as she is ready to move forward with her life—her life with Brett.

She rounds the path to the creek, dismounts and ties Lady to an old oak. Removing her hat, she stands on the edge of the bank looking for crayfish and listening to the trickle of water over the rocks green with moss. She splashes some of the cool water on her neck and forearms before turning her attention to the land bordering the creek and the lake and to the stakes with their small pink ribbons.

She tries to recall the architectural drawings as to the location of the rooms and the porches. Walking the property brings her a sense of satisfaction and it is the first feeling of peace she has known since leaving the hospital. It was a good idea for her to ride to this place. She finds a patch of grass in the shade, sits, and takes in a deep breath. Closing her eyes, she takes in her surroundings with her other senses: the musty smell of the creek, the birds chirping, the sound of leaves dancing in the breeze and the feel of the soft ground beneath her. A new sense of calmness emerges, and for the first time since the loss of her baby, it feels like she can go on. She is home.

CHAPTER 15

The feeling of tranquility acquired from her respite in nature is lasting, giving Gabby strength and a sense of purpose. On her ride back to the ranch, a thought suddenly makes her pull the reins hard. After Lady comes to a halt, Gabby turns the mare in the direction of the family cemetery, only a mile or so from this fork in the path. Even though she is thirsty and tired, she has a deep-seated desire to visit the baby she lost. She missed attending the small impromptu funeral her daddy arranged just a day after she was discharged from the hospital, when she was too weak to venture out. She will have to face seeing Jacob's gravesite sooner or later, so today is as good a day as any.

How can she visit her son empty-handed? Along the trail, she dismounts, gathering some daisies in the shade, still wet from the morning dew. The drops resemble her tears and she lowers her face into the delicate petals as if they are sharing this moment with her.

Now as she mounts her horse, the urge to turn around is strong.

She lowers her eyes and fights a sudden wave of nausea. Can she do this?

The cemetery is enclosed in a simple, black wrought-iron fence with a gate anchored by two cement pillars. Generations of the King family are buried here among the large oaks. A small fresh grave stands out amid the heavily grassed areas in front of the tombstones of her ancestors. After opening the gate and feeling spooked by its groaning hinges, Gabby approaches Jacob's grave and falls down as though her knees gave way. With an unsteady hand, she places the daisies on the sod with its few blades of tender grass, then she reaches out with her forefinger to trace each letter and number on the engraved stone, resting on the date of death. Closing her eyes, her dream of holding her little one resurfaces.

With tears streaming down her cheeks, her eyes search the heavens, visible between the boughs of the surrounding aged oaks, and she questions, "Why, God, why?" Not expecting an answer, she feels some relief just from the asking.

Then she looks to her mother's grave and whispers, "Please take care of him...until I get there."

Her hands brush the ground in an attempt to touch him, but this is futile, and she lowers her head and exhales as though her warm breath might penetrate the ground and in Jacob's sleep he may sense her presence. She wishes that he will dream of their precious moment together and he will feel her love.

As she stands, it's hard to catch a breath and her heart races. She must leave this place. *Was I crazy to come here?* She runs as fast as she can, hearing the gate slam behind her. Bringing Lady to a full gallop, she rides trying to get far away from the cemetery but also as far away as possible from the pain. This same pain that has engulfed her these past weeks has returned. She thought with time it would hurt less. She was feeling so peaceful and energized, eager to start over. She thought she was ready. Now she rides like a mad woman as if danger abounds. Is there no escape?

Minutes later, with a flushed face and tear-stained cheeks, she slows Lady to a walk. Throwing her shoulders back, she takes in a deep breath and lets it out with a sigh, as she nears the ranch and can see the peak of the barn just around the corner. She wipes her face before she leads Lady in the direction of the corral. Her intention is not to reveal the outcome of her visit to the cemetery to anyone.

Approaching the enclosure, it is as if a ray of light is shining through thick clouds and her face lights up. Brett, riding his brown quarter horse, has just roped a calf. She watches as he dismounts and uses the piggin' line that was clenched between his teeth to tie the animal's four hooves together. Rusty is seated on the fence with a stopwatch, yelling instructions.

Once more, she wipes her face with her dusty hand to help disguise any stains left by her tears. She smiles and waves to Brett. Guiding Lady up to the fence near Rusty, she sits and admires Brett's body as he works to untie the calf. The sleeves of his plaid shirt are rolled up to his elbows, exposing his bronzed firm arms, and the body of his shirt, wet with sweat, clings to his muscular form. Any girl would be lucky to call him her own.

He catches her stare and flashes a grin that deepens his dimple, and his bright green eyes tell her that he is glad she is there. She grins back and waves. How can she smile when she was so sad just minutes ago? This rollercoaster of feelings is confusing as well as exhausting.

Brett strolls across the corral to the fence and jumps as he swings his leg over the top railing and strides up to Lady. He pats the mare on her neck and then pulls on Gabby's arms so that she bends over toward him. He playfully gives her a kiss with just a tease of his tongue. She giggles and wraps a stray brown curl that is hanging below his hat around her finger. He smells of sweat and has dirt smudges on his face, but she is overjoyed to see him.

"God, I've missed you." He touches her face and she covers his hand with her own.

"I've missed you too. I didn't expect you to be back this early."

"Plans changed. You look flushed and you're warm. Do you feel okay?" She can read the concern in his eyes.

"I'm fine, just thirsty. I forgot to take water with me and I have been out a few hours." She looks down at her watch.

"That's not good. I'll get you a bottle from the barn."

Rusty pipes in, "Well, it looks like practice is over for today. You did good." He nods at Brett. "We'll meet tomorrow. Same time, got it?" He jumps off the fence. "I got work to do."

Gabby hops off Lady and pushes Brett up against the fence. "So show me how much you missed me."

"Don't you start something you can't finish," he says with a smile as he pulls her in tight.

"Oh, I can finish." She places her arms around his neck. Their kiss starts gentle and sweet but the passion builds as their tongues dance. She is the first to come up for air. Brett allows her to take a breath but then pulls her in again. She can feel his arousal and his hands leave her waist and grab onto her buttocks. She tries to push him away.

"Brett, you can't do that here."

He smiles at her and squeezes tighter.

"Daddy might see us."

"You said you could finish. Prove it." His eyes twinkle and his smile is wide.

"Later—I have work to do—water and feed Lady, then brush her down."

"Okay, later, you promise? Bet I can help you with Lady."

"I bet you can." She puts her arm around his waist. "Let's get that water."

Together they lead Lady up to the water trough, then into the barn. Gabby is quick to retrieve some water from the refrigerator near the office. After getting Lady settled, Brett takes Gabby's hand and backs her up against the stall.

"I do believe that it's later." There is a spark in his eye.

He leads her into an open stall and wraps his arms around her. "I leave for town in the morning," she gasps, trying to catch her breath.

He stands back. "What, tomorrow? Why?"

"Rita has me scheduled at ArtSmart, both shifts Friday and Saturday."

"You're kidding, right?"

"Wish I was. But guess I missed a lot of weekends and the new girl needs this weekend off." She looks down at her boots. "I do owe Rita. She's been great about everything. And she can't work because she needs to be here for Stan."

"But this weekend. When did she tell you?"

"Just this morning."

"Timing sucks. I've got things to do here. People are counting on me...Rusty, your dad. Can't you talk to her?"

"She was pretty adamant. I'm really sorry, Brett."

He cups her chin with his hand and searches her brown eyes. "I'm coming with you."

"You can't do that."

"Yes, I believe that I can. I won't have you going alone. I'll get in some serious practice time when I get back. I want to be with you, Gabby. Don't you want to be with me?"

"Of course I do, silly. But Daddy will be angry if you come with me. We both know that."

"Too bad, what's he gonna do? Fire me?" He shakes his head. "Hey, I don't want to talk about any of that now. I want to hold you. Be with you." He kisses her neck. "I've missed you. I've missed us."

Before she can protest he picks her up, carries her to the fresh hay and starts to caress her back with his hands. Through the denim she can feel his strength. His fingers are working their magic and her body trembles under his touch. She closes her eyes and gives out a moan. She has missed this man.

He unbuttons her blouse and slides his hands under her bra. Her breath quickens and she runs her fingers through his brown locks. When he unbuckles her jeans, she lifts her hips off the hay for him to easily slide her jeans to her knees. The desire to have him inside her overtakes reason. She doesn't wish to think. She needs to feel alive, to feel love. She wants to forget the pain of the past. He is quick to mount her and he groans with delight. Then it's as if someone gives him a gentle reminder that this is their first time since the accident.

His earlier greed is replaced now with a thoughtful, slower pace meant for her pleasure.

She feels he is teasing her with his meticulous movements and she begs him to move faster. In her passion she grips the muscles of his back, urging him to match her own quick movements. The waves of passion make her dizzy and she has difficulty remaining quiet, as small staccato vocal sounds escape from her throat. His confident smile shows he realizes that the power of his touch still drives her crazy.

"You feel great," he says. "Come with me."

He rolls to his side and strokes her with his hand. Spasms of release send waves through her body. He rolls on top again and drives deeper and harder. Her orgasm is almost more than she can bear and she arches her back as she grips more tightly. Brett places his hands under buttocks, lifting her up to meet his thrusts. After his climax he lies next her, breathing in and out in a slow rhythm.

"Wow," he says, hugging her shoulders.

"Wow," she responds, "that was incredible."

"Brett, Gabby." They hear Rusty call as he walks toward the main house. "King is pretty set on folks getting to dinner on time." They both giggle.

"We shouldn't have done this here. It's embarrassing." Quick to stand, Gabby pulls up her jeans and carefully tucks in her shirt, then runs her fingers through her hair, shaking out some pieces of hay.

"You seemed to enjoy yourself." He looks up, tilts his head and gives her a wink. "Rusty is well aware that you're not a little girl anymore. He wasn't born yesterday." After getting dressed, Brett takes her in his arms. He pushes a loose strand of hair away from her face and gives her a kiss. "It's mighty kind of Rusty to keep us on your daddy's good side. Let's go, princess, and clean up a bit before supper."

He kisses her once again before turning toward the bunkhouse. She brushes the hay off her jeans one last time, skipping toward the ranch house.

As she approaches the porch, she sees a wheelchair in the shadows and Stan calls to her.

"There you are. I've been waiting for you." He has a beer in his hand. He makes a motion with the bottle, waving it toward the barn. "I saw you and Lady go by close to an hour ago. I got you a glass of wine but it's warm now."

She can feel the heat in her cheeks and is unable to face his stare.

"What took so long? I know Brett was practicing." He points to the fresh cement supporting the stakes for the ramp. "Once this ramp gets finished, I'll be able to wheel myself right down there. I could watch. Maybe I could learn a thing or two." He smirks and his voice has taken on a sarcastic tone.

She pushes past him. "Sorry, Stan, but I have to wash up." Hurrying to get out of his view, she slams the screen door behind her and runs up the stairs.

Once safe in the confines of her room, Gabby looks in the mirror. *God, I am a mess.* Her cheeks are flushed and her hair is knotted. The afterglow of sex is obvious, she realizes, and the heat ignites in her cheeks again, turning them a deeper shade of scarlet. It wasn't in Stan's character to speak to her in that fashion. She backs up against the wall and swings the trinity knot on the chain around her neck back and forth.

Gripping the charm tightly and feeling as if it's speaking to her, she lifts her head. *This is for the best. A picture paints a thousand words. Maybe now he'll back off. It should be clear to him that I have chosen Brett. He needs to move on.*

CHAPTER 16

The sound of the dinner bell is cause for alarm. Her riding clothes hit the floor and she dons a pink sundress. After running a brush through her hair, she twists the blond strands into a knot and secures them with a clip. With haste she washes her face with a damp cloth and applies minimal makeup, making sure to use lipstick and some mascara to widen her eyes.

"Gabby, dinner," King yells.

"I'll be right there." She applies Chanel perfume to her neck and wrists. *This will have to do, instead of a much-needed shower.*

Stealing one last glimpse in the mirror, she turns, satisfied with her transformation and skips down the stairs.

In the living room, familiar faces turn to the curved staircase. With a smile, she boldly walks up to her daddy and plants a kiss on his cheek before finding her place beside Brett. He smells of soap and is wearing a fresh pair of jeans and a crisp white cotton shirt with the sleeves rolled up to his forearms. How has he managed to sparkle in so little time?

He hands her a glass of white wine, then plants a kiss on her lips as he places his arm around her. She reciprocates, reaching around his waist. Surveying the others gathered, she realizes that she has missed Stan's initial reaction to seeing Brett and vice versa. It was probably for the best, but she is curious as to how it all went down. Tonight will be difficult for all of them, but as her daddy had said earlier, if they are going to be a family, they need to work through this and the sooner the better.

Stan's wheelchair is beside the couch where Rita is sitting. In front of the fireplace, Rusty stands next to King and the two men seem to be engaged in deep conversation. She can hear sounds coming from the kitchen sending signals that Jamie is catering to the final details of their dinner.

Stan's eyes meet hers and she is quick to turn away.

King lifts his glass and clears his throat. "Now that Gabby has decided to join us, I want to give a toast...to family."

As she glances toward Stan, their eyes meet again and he lifts his glass as if toasting only to her. She gives a brief but awkward smile before returning her attention to Brett, distracted by the clicking of their glasses.

"To family," Brett says.

"To family," she repeats before taking a sip, savoring the coolness of the wine. "How did it go between you and Stan?" she whispers in Brett's ear.

"We were polite but it's clear we share a mutual hatred for each other." He lifts his eyebrows. "You can't expect us to be best buds." He straightens her necklace and his warm breath leaves moisture on her cheek.

"Daddy would like the two of you to be friends," she whispers as she squeezes his bicep.

"Hard for us to be friends. And if he doesn't stop staring, I swear I'm gonna go over there and punch him."

"Brett, don't play into his hand. He wants everyone to believe you have a temper and that you're a bully." She looks up with a stern face. "He's testing you. Ignore him. Look at me."

Brett shrugs his shoulders. "As usual, you're right. But I don't trust him, Gabby."

"You don't have to trust him, but you can trust me." She tugs on his arm, which makes him smile. "Daddy invited you here tonight because you're part of this family. If you're part of the family, well, that makes Stan your family, like it or not. You don't have to like him, just tolerate him. Okay? Can you do that for me?"

"I'll try, promise." He crosses his heart with his hand.

She stands on the balls of her feet and stretches to kiss him on the cheek and whispers, "Thank you." With this gesture, she realizes that in her haste, she has forgotten her shoes.

After the toast, the small group meanders into the dining room. Around the table, Gabby sits next to Brett, but Stan wheels to the chair on her left. It's the seat at the corner of the table so he can elevate his casted leg on a stool. Without help, he stands, pivots, and sits in the dining room chair.

"Stan, you're maneuvering much better," says King.

"Yes, I've learned to pivot while balancing this heavy cast so getting up and down is easier. Practice makes perfect, so they say. I can even get on and off the toilet all by myself." He pats himself on the back.

"Stan, that's way too much information. We're at the table." Rita rolls her eyes.

"I was just informing everyone here of my wonderful progress." He laughs.

King does not seem amused. Gabby wonders how she got sandwiched between Brett and Stan. Maybe that is better than the alternative, though. If those two sat next to one another, someone might end up with a fork stabbed into his hand. She shakes her head and thinks, *boys*.

Stan bangs on his arm cast. "In two more weeks I get this baby off and then I can use crutches. Hopefully the bones will be aligned in my knee so I can begin to bear some weight and get rid of this damn wheelchair."

Rita shakes her head. "Stan, don't swear at the table. Where are your manners? Did you leave them up on that mountain?"

Stan opens his mouth as if to respond but doesn't. In the meantime, Jamie and Rusty emerge from the kitchen carrying platters steaming with sliced barbecued brisket, fresh corn on the cob from the garden, and homemade corn muffins with bits of jalapenos.

After Jamie and Rusty take their places at the table, King reaches out for Rita's hand. "Time for grace." He has never missed giving thanks for his supper and waits patiently for all to participate by the joining of hands. Gabby readily takes Brett's hand and then is startled as Stan pulls her hand close to him and gives a hard squeeze as if demanding her attention. She turns in his direction, forces a smile before bowing her head and closing her eyes.

Grace is quick and to the point. Afterward, it takes her some effort to loosen Stan's grip as he holds on tight long after the "Amen" left her daddy's lips. *Stan is so annoying. Is he pouting now?* She reads sadness on his face.

At first the dinner conversation is polite with long periods of silence; however, whether it's the wine flowing or the family overcoming the initial awkwardness, everyone slowly begins to seem more at ease. That's when Gabby notices that Stan starts to monopolize the conversation. He always has a knack for storytelling and adds bits of humor, embellishing the truth, so that soon he has everyone laughing to the point of hysterics. Even Brett seems to relax a bit and laugh along with the others.

However, when Stan's outrageous narratives turn to the topic of Gabby's time spent in D.C. that spring, she leans back in her chair and nervously taps on her wine glass. *Where is he going with this?* She sucks in a deep breath and catches a glimpse of Brett's profile. She is not alone in her thinking, as she can see that Brett is biting his cheek. She scans the others at the table checking to see if there's a shift in their demeanor as well. She senses concern on her daddy's face, but Jamie, Rusty and Rita all seem fine.

Stan continues with one of his stories that he's changed so much Gabby has a hard time recognizing the event he is describing, even though she was there at the time. His voice is animated and his eyes are bright; he seems to thrive on all the attention he's receiving.

"It was a beautiful evening, almost perfect," Stan says. "The stars were shining. Even with the ambient light from the city, the stars were incredible." He waves his arm in the air as if trying to reach the heavens, then pauses and gives a nod in Gabby's direction before continuing. "Gabby, always the star-gazer." He chuckles and pats her hand.

Brett makes a sound clearing his throat.

She holds her breath and braces herself for what Stan may say next.

"We," he pauses for a sip of wine, "were in the backseat of the taxi and Gabby leaned in close and—"

"Stop." Her heart is racing and she can feel the heat in her face. "That's not exactly the way it happened." Every face is staring at her and there is silence.

With a gleam in his eye, Stan rests back in his chair as if lounging and plays with the stem of his wine glass. "Really, not right? So why don't you tell the story, Gabriella, since I've seemed to have remembered it incorrectly?"

"It, it...it really isn't worth mentioning. It was nothing." She stares him down. He was doing a great job at baiting her and she was being lured into his trap. She needs to be careful. It would be best for her to take the advice she gave to Brett earlier. *Don't take the bait. He wants to cause trouble between me and Brett.*

In the seconds it takes her to think, he starts in again. "Oh, yes, it was something." He nods his head up and down, exaggerating the motion. "We were in the back of the taxi coming home from the dance. You leaned in—"

She stares at him in disbelief. "I said stop." This time she is aware that she has raised her voice. It's as if time stands still. All are staring at her but none of those stares match the rage that is burning in Brett's eyes. Too late to take her words back, her anger turns into guilt and shame. She lowers her head and tears cloud her sight.

Pushing her chair back from the table, she stands and rubs her forehead. "I'm sorry. I don't mean to ruin everyone's dinner." She avoids looking at Stan. "I need to pack for the weekend."

"Where are you going?" King asks with a look of concern.

"I'm working Friday and Saturday at ArtSmart." She glances in Rita's direction and catches King also staring at his wife as if expecting an explanation.

"Isn't that a bit much for your first time back?" he asks.

"I'm behind on my weekend shifts. It's about time I work my fair share." She pushes her chair under the table. Meanwhile, Brett also stands. "Brett, walk out with me." She gives a nod toward the front door.

"Excuse us," Brett says, addressing Jamie and King. "Thank you for dinner. It was delicious as always."

CHAPTER 17

O nce they are out on the porch, Gabby is the first to speak. "The nerve of that guy." She crosses her arms in front of her chest. Brett follows her as she stumps down the steps and walks toward the barn before stopping at the fork.

He has his hands on his hips. "What did happen in the back seat of that taxi, Gabby? I thought that there was nothing between you and Stan. From the way you explained it, it was all Stan's doing but he seems to imply—"

"There you go, falling for his tricks. He wants us to fight. It's his intent to break us up. Please, Brett, don't let him win." She rubs his arms. "Please."

"I'd really like to know, exactly what did happen? Tell me. You owe me that much. How am I to fight when I don't know what I am up against?"

"Nothing happened...nothing. He wants you to believe that we had a thing. He did this all on purpose. Can't you see that?" Her eyes are pleading and she needs him to hold her and tell her that he loves her.

But he doesn't reach out for her. "If you are so innocent, why did you stop him?"

His intense stare scorches her soul. When she doesn't give him an answer, he continues, "You were afraid that I would hear that you made out with him and you had to hush him. Did you kiss him? Have sex with him? Is that it?"

She can't face him. *He's being ridiculous. How can he be thinking those things?*

"Do you think if I heard what he had to say I would walk away? Not love you anymore?" He runs his fingers through his hair. "I really don't understand. I know that you have been through a hard time here. I've tried to be supportive, patient, and understanding. I have been by your side through it all, but grow up, Gabby. It's time to be an adult."

"That's not fair! You have no idea what I've been through." She jerks her hand away and stares out into the distant horizon. "Today, when I was out riding Lady to see the land for our house, I went to the gravesite. I visited our son. That's what I have been doing. I'm trying to move forward by putting the past behind so I can look to our future. I've been trying to make sense of everything that has happened. I visited our son. Can you even fathom how hard that was for me?"

"He wasn't our son. He was your son...your son with Richard." His tone is harsh and it hits her in the gut like a brick.

She turns white, drops her head into her hands and sobs, "He was our son. We named him after your father. You said you could love him and raise him as your own. Was that all a lie?" Bending forward, she releases small muffled moans. Can he sense how his words hurt her?

He turns toward her. "I'm sorry, Gabby. I shouldn't have said that. I'm angry. I'm angry when I think of you with Richard and now, with Stan." He pushes her hair away from her face. "I'm sorry." He reaches out to hold her.

"Don't touch me. You should go." She pushes him away.

"Come on, Gabby. You said it yourself, don't let him win. I'm sorry. I shouldn't have said that. Whatever is in the past doesn't matter."

She lowers her head. "Please go. Okay? I can't do this now. It's too difficult." She turns and starts to walk at a fast pace toward the house.

He runs after her. "I'm sorry. I didn't mean it."

"It'll do us both good to think this thing through. I'm going to town tomorrow. You stay here. I'll call you."

"Gabby, really? Don't leave like this. Stay, talk to me. I apologized." He stands with his hands open in front of him.

"I can't, just can't. Forgive me." She turns and runs onto the porch.

Bang! She has hit something hard.

"Ouch," she yells as she rubs her leg. In the dark, she has tripped over the leg of Stan's wheelchair and she is certain that he intentionally blocked her path.

"Whoa there, cowgirl," Stan says. "Careful, you're gonna kill yourself."

Still rubbing her leg, with clenched teeth she says, "You're lucky I don't kill you first." She raises her hand as if to strike.

He reaches up, grabs her arm, and pulls her face, wet from her tears, within inches of his. "Temper, temper—it wasn't me who lost it in there."

"Let me go. I know what you're trying to do." She jerks her arm out of his hand and glares at him. She can't remember the last time she was this angry. Her tears disappear.

"Oh, really, what might that be, please tell?" His voice is teasing and she wants nothing more than to wipe that smug look off of his face. Without pausing for her to answer, he says, "You're a little wildcat. That comes as a surprise. It makes you even more appealing. Oh, the things I could do to you."

"You're disgusting," she snaps.

"Hey, keep your voice down. Maybe you want an audience? You like the drama—does it get you off?"

He has caught her off-guard. Her mouth is open but she has no words.

He laughs at her helplessness. If her looks could kill, he certainly would be dead.

In a quiet voice, a little more than a whisper, he says, "Gabriella, you are so blind. You're blinded by the romance, the sex. It will all be short-lived. You don't belong with him."

"You're such an ass." She hisses through clenched teeth.

"He isn't what you need. It hurts to see you throwing yourself at him. I'm at a disadvantage here in these casts and in this chair." He bangs on the armrests of the wheelchair. "Look at me, Gabby. Maybe, just maybe God caused this accident and brought me here so I can keep you from making the biggest mistake of your life."

She gives a high-pitched laugh. "Oh, so now you're bringing God into this. There's just no end to how low you'll stoop."

"Let's start over." He makes a gesture with his arm. "I'm willing to forgive you."

She gasps and leans back. "You're forgiving me?" She furls her brow and crosses her arms across her chest. "And why are you forgiving me?" Her mind is swirling. This conversation is crazy.

"For leaving me. I would have been there for you. I would have been there for the baby. Look what has come of this. You lost the baby. You should have stayed with me." He sucks in a deep breath. "You can't tell me you're happy. You and Brett fight all the time. It's okay to admit you made a mistake. We can start over."

"There was never a 'we,' and how can you sit there and bring up the loss of my baby as if it was my fault. You've got some nerve."

He reaches up for her hand. "You're confused. You've had too much to drink. We'll talk tomorrow when you are thinking more clearly."

She yanks her hand away. "You sound like the drunk here. I had no idea that you could be so mean." She puts her hands on her hips. "Is this Stan, Stan the lawyer, rearing his ugly head? Is that it? Using every argument, whether it's rational or not—God's will, alcohol, playing the victim with a heart full of forgiveness. Did I miss anything, Mr. Attorney?"

"You missed that I love you. Gabby, even with all of your faults, I still love you."

She looks at him in disbelief. "You're disgusting." She pushes past him and heads into the house, slamming the screen behind her.

In her room, seated at her vanity, Gabby brushes her long blond hair. *Damn, why are we fighting again?* This day has been an emotional rollercoaster. She started the day with a positive attitude, determined to move forward. In the morning she worked hard, forging ahead, making plans for their engagement party and her gallery exhibit. Then she went horseback riding, visiting the site of their future home. She braved the cemetery. Yes, that was difficult but necessary. And she has survived. Not as well as she would have liked; however, she did face the grave and had words with God.

This afternoon, her spontaneous rendezvous with Brett in the barn was sensational—and more. It was as if her life was going back to normal. She felt alive and strong. Making love with Brett had overshadowed her grief. He was gentle and patient but full of desire. His touch made her forget. Now, after working hard to take a step forward, she has slid back two.

How could Brett say those terrible things? He said he was sorry but could he not accept Jacob as a son?

Sighing, she stops brushing her hair and stares at her reflection in the mirror. The dark shadow that has been chasing her for the past few weeks is closing in again. After gaining some distance by actually finding some rays of happiness, the sadness nears, pulling at her soul, and the grief weighs her down. Does she have the energy to jump this hurdle? Her hand's unsteady and the brush seems as heavy as a brick.

Gabby searches the face in the mirror and frowns. *Maybe I don't deserve to be happy.* After putting down the brush, she reaches out for the photograph in the corner of her mirror. The smiling couple is a much-needed reminder that she and Brett were once a happy couple. Can they be happy again in spite of the challenges they face today? Is this just another detour or a dead end?

She's tired of detours and rocky roads. Two Bible passages come to her mind: "Do not grow weary. Win the race to receive your prize." Persist she must. Perhaps she did overreact at dinner. Why did she allow Stan to bait her?

Her thoughts drift back to her conversation with Stan and his harsh words. What was his intent? If it was to make him more endearing to her, he has failed miserably. If she had allowed him to continue his story, what could he have possibly said? They never even shared a mutual kiss, so why was she so quick to react? Would he have lied? She had done nothing in that taxi to cause herself embarrassment, so why does he put her on edge?

There are no re-dos in this life, just a chance to pick oneself back up and try again. In hindsight, she overreacted, but nothing can change that now. Brett also made a mistake when he denied Jacob as his son. He spoke out in anger. She knows his heart. Brett needs a re-do, too. They both said things that they regret. Propping her elbow on the vanity, she rubs her forehead. *I'll need to make this up to him.*

Earlier this year, she had lived with Stan for two months. He had been her rock during one of the most difficult times of her life, and in all that time, he never spoke a mean word. He even offered to be a father to her son. By choosing Brett, did she hurt Stan so much that he turned into this bitter, angry, unrecognizable creature? Is it the accident and the long recovery that is making him act out? Certainly, his current behavior is puzzling. What's really going on with Stan?

Before closing the drawer, Gabby remembers a family ring she had placed there for safekeeping years ago. Digging back into the far corner of the drawer, her fingers grasp the small box. Setting the ivory box in front of her, she opens it and there, gleaming on red velvet, is her grandmother's ring.

The story has it that when her grandparents married, they barely had two pennies to rub together, but with hard work they were able to get by. When in town one day buying supplies for the ranch, her granddaddy met a visitor who had run into troubled times. The man needed a horse to get him to El Paso. After sharing a beer with the stranger, listening to his sad tale, her granddaddy had empathy for the man and traded one of his good horses for the only thing of worth the man owned, this ring. It has been in her family ever since. Her grandmother passed the ring down to Gabby's mother, Anna. When Anna died, Gabby became the ring's owner but she has never worn it, as it was too big for her small fingers and she feared losing it. She tucked it away in this drawer and had almost forgotten that it was there.

She holds the ring and smiles as it sparkles under the vanity light. She slips it onto her left hand and spins it around, watching the shine of large center diamond and the golden band with intricate carvings of leaves that encircle it. As a young girl, Gabby always admired the ring. Why didn't she bother to get it resized? Tilting her head to the side, she studies the ring, liking the way the stone sits low in the setting.

She lets out a deep breath and nods in approval before carefully placing the ring back in the box. Then, instead of putting the box back in the drawer, she slips it into her purse. It is a shame that this ring has lived in a dark drawer; it needs to see the light of day. *Hide it under a bushel, no. I'm gonna let it shine.*

CHAPTER 18

If Gabby had stayed downstairs, she would have seen Stan smile from ear to ear as he was pleased with their confrontation.

He may not be a practicing attorney anymore but he's still capable of manipulating the witness and the jury. It was dark, too dark to see past the porch, but Stan had hopes that Brett had seen him and Gabby together. He wanted her to lower her voice so that, if by chance Brett was listening, he would think that they were having an intimate after-dinner chat. Stan searched the heavens as he guzzled his wine. Were the stars aligning for him?

Back in the makeshift bedroom, he winces in pain as he struggles to lift his body out of the wheelchair and pivots on his good leg to get into the bed. *Ouch, this damn leg.* Moments earlier he had felt so good, having accomplished his goal. His performance had caused Brett and Gabby to be angry with each other.

He frowns. How dare Gabby stroll up the driveway this afternoon looking like she had a roll in the hay? Damn, he was furious when he saw her. He'd waited on the porch for hours, concerned that something bad had happened when she was out riding. She didn't answer his text messages or his calls. He needed to teach her a lesson, but now he shakes his head. He feels like a jerk. Did he go too far?

There's a knock at the door. "Stan, honey, do you need any help?"

"No, Mother, doing fine, thanks." He hears her steps get farther away. "Good night," he calls after her.

Lifting his prescription bottle of hydrocodone, he pops a few of the pills in his mouth and washes them down with wine from the glass he managed to stow between his legs and not spill. When he finishes this glass, he will start on the flask with tequila that he was able to fill from the bar earlier.

He recalls his conversation on the porch with Gabby, when she called him disgusting and an ass. He had never heard her swear before. He had always thought her to be level-headed. He shakes his head. What was wrong with her?

An ache in his leg diverts his attention. God, he wishes this pain would go away. He drains the last of the wine. *Damn, I'll need to get out of the bed to get the flask out of the dresser.* He should have put it on the bedside stand. Maybe he'll just wait here until the pills take effect before making the pilgrimage across the room to the dresser.

Moments later, the room is turning and his head is spinning. How many pills did he take? He tries to prop his elbow on the nightstand and reach for his crutch with his good arm but he is dizzy, loses his footing and falls to the floor. His pride hurts more than his leg so he refuses to call out for help. After a while, facing the fact that he isn't physically capable of getting back on the bed without help, he pulls a pillow and blanket from the bed. *My life sucks.*

He shouldn't have challenged Gabby. Tonight, she was right

about many things. He was using every possible angle, but it was low for him to insinuate that she had lost the baby because she left him. And it was small to voice that it was God who caused his accident so that he could get closer to her. Maybe she was right that he is disgusting...and an ass.

How has it come to this? He was always in control. He was smart. Now, he is pathetic, he hurts and the pain is relentless. Loneliness will be his friend tonight as Gabby pretty much seems to hate him. He closes his eyes, aware that he is a desperate and fallen man.

PART III

CHAPTER 19

A rtSmart has had a busy day. That's typical for a Friday in Austin and it's a good thing as it keeps Gabby's mind off her long list of problems. However, now an hour before closing with only one customer in the gallery, Gabby takes off her shoes and rubs her swollen feet. It would be nice to lie down on the couch in the back, put her feet up, and take a nap. This eight-hour shift her first day back has taken more of a toll on her than she anticipated.

She scratches her head and picks up her phone but the screen is blank. Earlier that morning, she had both called and texted Brett. Still, there is no response. Her shoulders slump as she hangs her head. *Why are we always fighting?* She debates the idea of trying again. *When Brett has time he will call. He will apologize.*

She remembers that today Rusty expected Brett to practice his tie-down technique for the rodeo. The competition is only one week out, and maybe he has been busy, as Rusty and her daddy are counting on him. She's aware that he feels the pressure to do well, so reluctantly she puts the phone back on the counter. He doesn't need additional pressure coming from her. *He's just busy.* She rubs her forehead and sighs.

All of this drama in her life reminds her of her best friend, Ella, who recently married Stan's brother, Will. Drama always seemed to follow Ella. In college, they were sorority sisters and quickly became close. On numerous occasions, Gabby was the one giving advice about relationships to her distraught friend. Her fingers race to retrieve Ella's contact information. Ella will make her laugh and think it funny that the tables have turned and that it's Gabby who's in need of advice. The call goes to voice mail and she waits for the beep. "Hey, girlfriend, we are overdue for a long chat. Call me back."

The bells on the gallery door jingle, but Gabby, preoccupied with the paperwork required for closing, doesn't glance up as she speculates that her only customer has just left the store.

After opening the door to allow the woman to exit ArtSmart, Brett takes a moment to search the gallery for Gabby. He finds her standing at the register and it is obvious that she hasn't paid any attention to the sound of the bells. He pauses to catch his breath and his heart skips a beat. It still amazes him that he has landed this beautiful woman. The corners of his mouth turn up as he watches her working intently.

He runs through a mental inventory, remembering the women he hooked up with before dating Gabby. None of them came close to making him feel this way. Back then, when he worked as a tennis pro, he was a reckless playboy. So much has changed in the past few months. And if this weekend goes as he anticipates, many more changes will happen in the near future.

He reminds himself that whatever transpired between Stan and Gabby is old history. With his own past, he's in no position to judge. And it really doesn't matter—what does matter is that he and Gabby are engaged and they will be spending forever together. He isn't going to allow some self-serving jerk in a wheelchair to gain empathy by manipulating them and provoking arguments to try and destroy what he and Gabby have worked hard to achieve.

Back in D.C. this summer, Gabby made her choice and picked him. Now it is time for Brett to man up. He's going to claim what is his and Stan isn't going to like it.

Earlier today at the ranch

After practice in the corral, Brett had followed King into the barn and found him seated at the desk.

"Ahhh, Mr. King, can I have a word with you?" Brett licked his lips and wrung his hands.

"Yes, oh, good, Brett, glad you're here." King scooted his chair back from the desk and placed his pen behind his ear. "Hey, I want you to take a few days off; all work and no play isn't good, rest up a bit because next weekend is the big event in Waco. I'll have Rusty time a few of your tie-downs closer to the end of the week but, Brett, you worked really hard these past few days. Take this weekend off. You earned it."

"Thank you, sir. I sure do appreciate it." Brett took off his cowboy hat. "I need to speak with you about something. Well, ask you something, to be correct."

"What is it?"

"I would like to ask for Gabby's hand in marriage...sir."

"Aren't you already engaged?" King continued to look at the ledger in front of him.

"She asked me but I wanted to ask your blessing...hmm, well... before I make it official."

"Is that so?" King looked up smiling. Then he stood and patted Brett on the shoulder.

"I couldn't have asked for a better man to be my son-in-law. Of course you have my blessing. I know that many young folks think it's a bit old-fashioned to ask permission, but I appreciate the formality."

"Thank you, sir, thank you." Brett sighed in relief.

"Now get out of here. Get to town before rush hour." King smiled. "It will be good for you to get away for a few days. Spend some time together and away from all the messy stuff going on here."

Thinking about that conversation makes Brett stand tall now, as he gazes at the woman he loves with flowers in his hand, permission from her daddy in his back pocket and an apology on his lips. Everything, once fixed, will be great. Throwing his shoulders back, and smiling from ear to ear, he approaches the register. "Excuse me," he says.

Gabby jumps and places her hand on her chest. "Sorry, you startled me. I didn't hear you come in." His wide smile makes his dimple more pronounced and she offers a smile that matches his, then points to the potted plant he's holding.

He hands her the flowers. "I thought we could plant these near Jacob's grave. The woman at the garden shop thought that zinnias would hold up well over the cooler winter months." He shifts his weight from one foot to the other. "I'm really sorry I said what I did last night. Jacob is our son, yours and mine. I was just angry. Stan has a way of setting me on edge."

"I'm sorry too. I hate when we quarrel. This is so thoughtful. It means a lot." She rolls the soft petal of a pink flower between her fingers. "This is really nice. I like it and I love you for thinking of Jacob. Thank you," she whispers.

He turns to kiss her. Her taste is sweet and he pulls her in closer, aware that the zinnias are being crushed. He doesn't care.

She's the first to pull away. "What are you doing here? Today is your day to practice."

"I impressed your daddy so much that he gave me the weekend off." He rocks his shoulders back and forth and places his hands on his hips. "He gave me R and R, so I chose to drive down here, take you out for a nice dinner and then we can spend the rest of the evening in bed."

She looks down at her dress. "Why didn't you tell me? I look a mess."

"That would have ruined my surprise. You look fabulous. I'm the luckiest man alive to have you as my dinner date." He flashes another killer smile in her direction as he runs his forefinger down her neck and catches the top of her dress causing more of her cleavage to be exposed. "We can skip dinner if you'd rather and go right to bed, your choice."

"What surprise?" she asks with her hand on her chin, avoiding answering his immediate question.

"If I told you, it wouldn't be a surprise, now would it."

She rolls her eyes, then looks at her watch. "It's about an hour before closing. Do you want to wait in the back? Rita keeps beer in the fridge."

"Tempting...but close early," he whispers in her ear as his hand caresses her butt.

"It's only four o'clock." She pushes his hand away.

"Close early," he whispers again, kissing her neck.

She shakes her head. "Rita will get angry."

He backs her up to the counter. "Rita will never know. Besides, you're already closed." He kisses her neck.

She pushes him away and her puzzled look makes him laugh.

"It was fortunate that the only customer in the gallery left when I was coming in, so I flipped the open sign to close and latched the door. You, princess, closed the shop about ten minutes ago."

"You are such a bad boy." She shakes her finger at him.

"But I'm a good man." He unzips her dress. As she turns to protest, he pulls her dress to her waist and his hands slide down her stomach and reach inside her lace panties.

She leans back into him and moans.

"I want you, now." He picks her up and carries her into the back.

"Wait," she says. "The lights."

He stops in the doorway and she flicks off the lights to the gallery. With her arms enclosing his neck as he places her on the couch, she pulls his lips toward hers and her hands start to unbutton his shirt. Sex was on the menu for tonight but it was supposed to happen later. He isn't opposed to having dessert before the main course. He grins. *It is a great idea.*

Later that evening, Brett holds open the door for Gabby and ushers her into the small jewelry store. The white-haired jeweler peers over his glasses, looking up from his work table. Recognizing Brett from his previous purchases, the owner eagerly walks toward them with his hand extended.

"Mr. Matthews, it's so good to see you again." The jeweler steps back after shaking Brett's hand and gives Gabby the once-over from head to toe as he clicks his tongue against the roof of his mouth and shakes his head. "It all makes sense now after seeing this beauty." He reaches out his hand. "It is a pleasure to finally meet you. Now I understand." He turns to Brett and pats him on the shoulder. "You're indeed a lucky man."

The jeweler looks back to Gabby. "I can see you're wearing the necklace. My best guess is that it was six months ago or so when I fixed that clasp. Time goes by quickly for this old man." He points to himself and smiles. "Oh, yes, then it was the bracelet."

Gabby instantly grabs her naked wrist. She has been unable to wear the bracelet since that night in the hospital. "I'm not wearing it today but I really love it." She makes an effort to show happiness with her tone but she wonders if she was successful. Truth is the bracelet has been hard for her to wear as it reminds her of Jacob.

She continues to stare at her wrist, not wanting to give the jeweler a chance to sense sadness in her eyes.

She sighs in relief when he asks, "So what can I do for you today?"

Brett takes a deep breath and places his hand in the small of Gabby's back. "Today is the day. It's time. We're here in search of an engagement ring."

"Happy day, congratulations! Helping a young couple pick out a ring is a joyous occasion." He claps his hands together. "Please, follow me this way." He turns and leads them to a large case in the corner and motions for them to sit on the two white-cushioned chairs.

"This section of the case has solitaire settings and the next section has bridal sets. Take your time. Each ring has its own personality. See what speaks to you." The jeweler places a dark blue velvet cloth on the top of the counter. "After you pick out a few, I'll gather them and tell you all about your selections. I'll be right back."

Brett reaches for Gabby's hand. "What do you think?" His smile is contagious and she smiles back.

"Wow, we're really doing this?"

He squeezes her hand again. "Yep, I got your daddy's permission this morning."

"You actually asked my daddy?" Her eyes are wide as if in disbelief.

"Yep."

"You really are serious, but I'm a bit surprised."

"Why is that?"

"Things haven't been going smoothly for us lately." She bites her lip. "I'm really sorry. I—"

He places his finger on her lips. "I'm sorry too. It's time to move forward. Do you still want to marry me?"

"Of course, I asked you first."

"Just checking, as you don't seem so sure now." He scans her face as if to validate her answers.

"I'm just surprised. We never talked—"

"Hey, let's do this." He turns away and focuses on the rings in the case. "I like this one." He points to a square diamond in a gold setting. "What do you think?"

She smiles. "It's nice." She wraps her arm around his. He leans into her, kissing the top of her head, which seems to chase away the lingering doubt that was weighing heavy on her mind.

A lighter heart accompanies a new mindset. This is going to be fun. She takes a deep breath and continues to hold onto Brett's arm, reminded that every girl dreams of this day.

"I love your surprises."

Gabby points to a round stone encircled by smaller stones. "I like this one."

"That's pretty," Brett says. "How about this one?" He points to an oval diamond.

The jeweler returns, carrying a silver tray with two flutes of champagne. "This calls for a celebration." He hands each a glass and says, "Here's to your future together."

They click their glasses before sipping the bubbly liquid.

"Show me what you selected and we'll get started." Moving behind the glass case and wearing his glasses, the older man retrieves the selected rings and displays them on the blue velvet cloth. Gabby anxiously places one of the solitaires on the third finger of her left hand. The band is too large and the diamond turns easily on her finger, but she likes the way the ring reflects the light. She returns it and then gives her attention to the round diamond surrounded by the smaller stones. It reminds her of the gem stowed away in her purse.

The jeweler is kind and patient. "You have quite a selection here—all different shapes and styles." He reaches for the ring sizer. "You look to be a size five and a half." He motions for her to place her finger into one of the many metal bands, and when it fits perfectly into the size five and a half, he says with a smile, "I've been doing this a long time, since before you were born."

One by one, she tries on the rings. "They are all so beautiful. How can I choose?"

"You'll know when you find it. Trust me."

Brett remains quiet.

"What do you think?" She holds out her finger adorned with the ring that has the large diamond surrounded by the smaller stones.

"It's really up to you. You're the one wearing it." He takes her hand. "I don't know much about any of this. Pick what you like."

An hour later, the jeweler has informed them about the carat weight, cut, color, and clarity of each stone in the rings that they picked, but each diamond's luster seems to dull when Gabby compares it to the treasured history that cut each facet of her grandmother's ring. She reaches for her purse and gives the jeweler a nod, asking, "Can we please have a moment?"

"Most certainly." He winks. "Let me clean this up."

After the old man returns the empty glass flutes to the silver tray and exits through the back curtain, Brett leans back in the chair, stretches and folds his hands behind his head.

"Lots of things to consider in making a decision," he says. "They're all nice. It's your choice."

She leans back in her chair as well so that she can watch his face. "I'm going to be honest with you, and I don't want to hurt your feelings."

He sits erect, his smile fading. "Should I be concerned?" His eyes dart back and forth, scanning her face. His panic causes her heart to sink.

"You need to have faith in me." Her voice has a teasing quality that seems to relieve his tension.

"What is it?" He wrinkles his brow. "I want us to be honest and open with each other...about everything."

She hands him the small ivory box. "Open it. This ring was my grandmother's. I love that you want to buy me an engagement ring but if you don't mind, I would like to use this one. Let's ask the jeweler about it." She motions toward the back of the store.

He holds the ring up to the light. "It is quite beautiful."

A few minutes later, they hear whistling and the jeweler returns. "Do you have any questions?"

"Yes, I do have one question. I have this family heirloom." She holds the ring for him to see. "It was my grandmother's. Can you please tell us more about it?"

The jeweler examines the stone with his loupe. Several minutes pass and he seems so engrossed with his inspection that Brett and Gabby look at each other, questioning whether they should disturb him.

Brett clears his throat. "Is it real?"

"Oh, it's real, no doubt about that." The man doesn't look up from his work. Another minute passes and then he says, "It's a European hand-cut diamond. Back in those days everything was hand-cut. And it's in a cathedral setting. This deeper cut is deceiving as it hides some of the diamond's weight. The color is great and the clarity is nearly perfect. I can't be sure but an educated guess is that this diamond's almost three carats. With this original hand-carved band, I would guess that it's worth six figures."

It's as if he can't peel his eyes away from the stone. Still inspecting, he says, "I'll need to do some research. This is quite an exquisite piece. I haven't seen one like this—well, only in books, of course, very interesting. How did you say your family came to own this?"

"My grandfather traded a horse for it."

The jeweler chuckles, "Your grandfather got the better end of the deal. It is more than one hundred years old. Hand-carved bands like this one were the style back in the eighteen hundreds."

Gabby glances over at Brett. She can see he is baffled as he is checking out the price tags on the rings left on the velvet cloth. Knowing none of them come close to the value of her grandmother's ring, she makes a mental note to explain the priceless value of sentimentality after they leave the store.

"I really love this ring. These others are beautiful but I would like to wear the ring that my mother and grandmother wore. You have been helpful showing us your rings and giving us champagne. We're really sorry to have taken up so much of your time."

"Not a problem, young lady. I enjoyed your company, and this ring, wow, a real pleasure just to hold it."

"Can you resize it?"

"Five and a half, of course." Then he asks, "Is this ring insured?"

"I don't know. I'll have to ask my daddy."

"It should be. I can appraise it. The insurance company will need that. It sure is a beauty. I can have the resized ring back to you by tomorrow but the paperwork will take a few more days. I'll make a few calls and talk to some antique dealers who know more about this than I would ever know. Sound good?"

"Perfect," Brett says as he pushes his chair back from the display case. Gabby follows suit. After shaking the man's hand, Brett is quick to walk to the front of the store as if he cannot get out of there fast enough. She turns to bid the jeweler goodbye and then as soon as the shop door closes, Brett says, "Your grandmother's ring is so expensive. I can't afford anything close to that."

She stands still. "Stop that, it's not about the price. It's about the sentimental value. You said it was my choice and I pick my grandmother's ring, the ring that has been in my family for three generations."

"Don't you think it should be in a safe?" Brett shakes his head.

"It just spent the last few years in my vanity drawer. It's high time to wear it and to let its beauty shine for all to enjoy."

"Hey, if you're happy, then I'm happy." She hears him sigh and wonders if that was a sign of relief that the task of the engagement ring was finished or that he has just dodged a hefty price tag.

"Good, I'm happy and starved. You promised me a nice dinner. Let's get going."

CHAPTER 20

The following morning Gabby tries to sneak out of bed, but Brett opens his eyes when her feet hit the floor.

"Go back to sleep," she says quietly. "I'm sorry if I woke you."

He squints as he lifts the blind to reveal the sky bathed in sunlight. "Too late, I'm already awake."

"I'm sorry."

"You'll have to come here and make it up to me." He holds his arms reaching out to her.

She walks around the bed and then leans over to give him a kiss and he grabs her, holding her down. "Brett, I'll be late for work."

"Do you have to go? It's a beautiful day. We could play tennis."

"Tennis? I sure could use the exercise."

"See, it's a perfect idea."

"Yes, perfect, except I have to work."

"Don't go in," he says and she notices that his dimple is more pronounced, which means that he is testing her.

"You closed the gallery early yesterday, remember? I need to be there today."

He flops back down on the bed. "Take along your tennis stuff. When I pick you up we'll go and hit a few balls at the club. It will be cooler then and also not as busy. We can grab some barbecue, go to the park and watch the sun set."

"That sounds delightful and romantic."

"Good, we have a plan. I'll pick up your ring while you're at work. Are there any other errands you need done?"

"You could get a haircut."

He looks at her with a furled brow.

"Our engagement party is in two weeks. I want you to be handsome for the photos, but with that dark tan you have from working outside, it would be best to get your hair cut today. Then you can tan that line of white skin around your neck and you won't look so dorky."

"Me, dorky, really?" He throws a pillow at her.

Laughing, she ducks. "And, Brett, does your tux fit? Even if it does, it needs to be pressed." He rolls his eyes. "I saw that. I'm just helping you." She puts her hands on her hips. "Try it on and then take it to the cleaners, after your haircut."

"You're going to have me busy all day. Today is my day off."

"Poor baby, I want our party to be perfect. These things have to be done. I can't get your hair cut for you."

"As always, you're right."

She stands naked in the bathroom doorway, grinning. "Since you're awake, you can shower with me. If I open the gallery a few minutes late, so what." She turns, flashing her firm buttocks in his direction as she disappears.

Quickly he hops out of bed. He doesn't want her to change her mind and the vision of her silhouette against the light of the bathroom reminds him that he likes her body more than her organizational skills. He would have never thought to get a haircut or to get his tuxedo pressed, but he's aware that the engagement party tied to Gabby's opening reception for her artwork will be an important evening. He wants to be at his best. Since, he, Brett Matthews, is engaged to Gabriella King, the most beautiful woman in the town. Smiling, his boxers slide to the floor before he jumps into the bathroom shower. *Oh, I'm a lucky man.*

"Wow, you got here fast." Gabby opens the passenger door to Brett's Audi that afternoon.

"It was a fortunate chain of events. I just finished running the errands when I got your text." He grins. "What was Rita's reaction when you informed her that the whole parking lot was flooded?"

"She already knew as the city called all of the store owners in the center." Gabby buckles her seatbelt.

"Good, then she knows that you're telling her the truth." He winks.

"Of course, I always tell the truth." She stops rummaging through her purse. "I just don't tell her everything."

"Like how you closed an hour early yesterday." He taps his fingers on the steering wheel.

"Correction, you closed early. I found out about it after the fact but, yes, Rita doesn't need to know that." After finding her sunglasses, she says, "It sure is hot. Anyway, like you said earlier, it's great that I had to close the store at noon because of the break in the main waterline. I'm excited that we're going to play tennis. I've missed that."

"I'm happy to spend time with you." He reaches over to caress her shoulder.

"That's so sweet. Me too. We need alone time without family around. It'll be wonderful to go to the club." She tilts her head. "Do you ever miss it?"

"Miss what, tennis?"

"Yes, teaching tennis and hanging out at the club. If I remember correctly, you got a lot of attention from the women. Do you miss that?" She looks out of the window and draws in her bottom lip. She never revealed how relieved she was when Brett traded his tennis racquet for the ranch as it did bother her when the women, especially her teammates, flirted with him.

"Sometimes, I miss it. I taught for years but I'd rather be at the ranch. At least that's how I feel today. In a few years, I may be thinking differently. Why do you ask?"

"I just wondered. We both made a lot of changes in our lives in a short period of time. I want you to be happy."

"I'm happy. Don't I seem happy?" He gives her a big grin, then sticks his tongue out between partially clenched teeth.

"I'm serious, Brett."

"Yes, seriously, I'm happy. Are you happy?" He pats her hand.

"Yes." She sits back into the seat and relaxes her shoulders.

"Good." He presses harder on the gas pedal and the car speeds down the road.

Pulling the car into a parking space at the tennis club a few minutes later, they grab their racquets from the trunk.

"It's going to be a hot one," Gabby says as she puts the bag's shoulder strap over her head.

"Changing your mind about playing?"

"Not a chance. I plan to whip your butt." She grins.

"Is that so?" He pulls her in close. "Want to put a wager on that? I know just what I want when I beat your cute little ass." His hand leaves her waist and grabs her buttocks.

She laughs. "You're so shallow. Men are so predictable." She rolls her eyes.

Before they reach the front door of the club, several players stop them, offering sentiments that they miss Brett and that the tennis center isn't the same since he left. Moments later, news of his arrival must have spread for when they check into the desk for their court assignment, the director of tennis comes out of his office to greet them. After inquiring about the ranch, the man doesn't hesitate to offer Brett a teaching job again.

Today she is certain Brett would not accept the job offer. She observes the way he stands tall and hears the firm tone in his voice when he speaks of the ranch and of his success on the rodeo circuit. From all the attention he is receiving, she is suddenly aware that although she is proud of him and appreciates that others also admire him, that wave of insecurity nags, suggesting that she will have to be careful or he could be snatched away. Her stomach churns.

Now, she stands close at his side and smiles. She reminds herself to take slow deep breaths in an attempt to quiet the inner turmoil. When they are at the ranch, everything is simple but here in town things seem complicated. What if he gets bored with the ranch or with her? Would their relationship be strong enough to survive? It is clear that he would have choices. Today he would choose "us" but what about all of the future tomorrows?

Nearly an hour passes before they walk to their tennis court and start to play. Within seconds of picking up the racquet, Brett hits the ball with skill and confidence, and it's as if he never took a break from the game. He bounces around on the court like a kid wearing a new pair of sneakers.

Even though he is hitting the ball straight to her and at half pace, she struggles as her timing is off and she's not bending her knees. Taking time away from the court has not been as kind to her tennis game. She tries to laugh, remembering that it is her first time back on the court in over four months. Even though she struggles, it's fun doing something familiar together.

With their court time soon over, Brett zings a few balls past her just to prove that he is still "the man" on the court.

"Show-off," she says, wiping the sweat from her brow. "You do look dorky with that white line around your neck. I'm glad you got a haircut today."

"So you concede losing to a dorky-looking guy?"

"I don't mind losing to a dorky-looking former tennis professional if that's what you are insinuating. Yes, you win. It's hot out here and

I'm so done." She reaches for her water bottle, and after taking a huge gulp she lifts her shirt away from her body and pours some of the cold water down her chest. "That feels nice. My game is so off."

"You're just out of practice. It'll come back. You conceded, so I get my wager, right?" His eyes gleam as he walks over to the bench near the middle of the court. He roots in his tennis bag and retrieves a small box. "Because you lost our little bet, you'll have to wear this."

She covers her mouth with her hands. "My ring, you had it all of this time."

He takes a knee and opens the box. "Gabby King, will you marry me?"

All the insecurities she previously thought about have vanished. "Yes, yes, a thousand times yes." She wraps her arms around his shoulders and hugs him tightly. He places the ring on her left hand.

"It's beautiful. I love it. I love you."

He lifts her feet off the ground and swings her around the court. "We're going to be so happy."

"We are already." Still in the air, she eyes the ring on her hand, admiring how it sparkles in the sunlight. *It is official, we're engaged.*

CHAPTER 21

Stan enjoys leisurely afternoons on the shady porch of the ranch house, especially after physical therapy and with a full stomach from one of Jamie's lunches. The slam of the screen door, followed by footsteps, rouses him from his daydream.

"Hey, sweetie, how's my boy?" His mother's words do not match her sharp tone. Her hands are on her hips.

He rolls his eyes before sitting up straight in his chair. "Just peachy."

She stands facing him. "How did therapy go today?"

"Fine, just fine."

"The therapist spoke with me on his way out. He thinks that you've given up—no motivation. There's been no noticeable improvement in the last few sessions." She waits for him to answer but Stan just shrugs his shoulders and looks away.

She takes a seat on the rocking chair next to him. "My Stan would want to be the best that he could be. Work hard and do what it takes."

He reaches for his glass and takes a gulp of the clear liquid.

"Well, what do you have to say? How can we help you?"

"There's nothing to do, Mother. It is what it is."

"I'm trying hard to understand. Tell me what's going on?"

"Nothing's going on. Maybe there isn't going to be any improvement." He takes another sip.

"I'm going to take this opportunity to remind you that you asked for my help." She places an empty pill bottle on the table. "After speaking with the therapist, I went through your room. Found this empty pill bottle and this empty fifth of vodka in the corner of the closet."

Stan rolls his eyes again. "You shouldn't be going through my things. The therapist is breaking the privacy act. He shouldn't be discussing my condition with you. I'll request someone else. I'll show him not to go behind my back."

"It wouldn't be in your best interest." She reaches for the glass on the table, smells the contents, and then stands and pours the remaining liquid over the edge of the porch.

"Hey, what are you doing?"

"Guess I got your attention now. The therapist says your pupils are pinpoint and you reek of alcohol. He can't work with someone in your condition. You're lucky he came to me and isn't reporting you." Rita sits down again. "I get it. You've been through a lot. The road to recovery is long and it's hard. PT is no picnic. I'm not making light of the pain you must be in, but these first months are crucial to your recovery. You want a full recovery, right?"

"Full recovery, yeah, right?" He shakes his head.

She touches his arm. "You could have died out there on that mountain. But you didn't. You survived. You could recover fully.

You need to strengthen your back. Get everything strong and in alignment so when you can put some weight on that leg, everything will work properly. Lying in bed for all those weeks in traction stole most of your muscle tone. You need to build up."

"Stop treating me like a child. I know what I'm doing. You worry too much."

"Worry about their children is what a mother does, Stan. This sort of thing, the pills and the alcohol can get out of hand in the blink of an eye." She squeezes his hand. "Stan, don't give up. Promise me you'll work hard. Lay off the alcohol and the drugs. You're better than this." She stands and gives him a hug. "I could have lost you back on that mountain. It would be devastating to lose you now." She kisses him on his forehead.

He rubs his forehead and listens for the slam of the screen door. How could he have been so careless? Still, she had no right to go through his room. His mother may be right about some things but not everything. The pain from his leg is nothing compared to the gaping hole in his heart. Every time he sees Gabby with Brett the hole bores deeper.

CHAPTER 22

Gabby stands in the doorway of the office in the barn. Since Stan is using the home office as a bedroom, King is forced to work here. "Hi, Daddy, I baked you cookies, your favorite." She hands him a plate of oatmeal raisin cookies that are chock full of chocolate bits. He flashes a huge grin.

"Wow, does Rita know about these?" He shoves a cookie into his mouth. "Ummm, ummm, she put me on a diet, you know. Thinks I'm getting a little soft." He pats his belly.

Gabby takes a seat on a chair on the other side of his desk.

"Jamie warned me as much but Rita's out. There is a women's luncheon over at the Conlee ranch."

"That's right. MaeLou was having a meeting about some fundraiser. Makes me happy that the other ladies are welcoming Rita into the community." He reaches for another cookie.

"Of course the ladies welcome Rita. She's a sweetie, not to mention that she has your money backing her. If MaeLou wants money to fund her charity, she's wise to include Rita." Gabby winks at him.

"Speaking of charities, I would like your help with an investment for a business venture."

He pushes his chair away from his desk and furls his brow. "Charity and business investments are two different things, my dear."

"I need your expertise and some additional funds to make it all happen." She leans back in the chair.

"Here I thought you were baking my favorite cookies because you appreciate your old man. Now, these tasty little morsels seem like a bribe." A twinkle appears in his eyes.

"A way to a man's heart is through his stomach. Mother taught me that. However, I do appreciate you and it's been a while since I made a batch of her cookies. It's fun to be in the kitchen with Jamie. Just like old times."

"Well, young lady, you certainly got my attention, but first things first. Hope this business idea doesn't have anything to do with Brett. The rodeo starts in a few days and I can't have my boy distracted."

"No, this has nothing to do with Brett. I wanted to discuss it with you first and I won't mention it to him until after the rodeo, promise." She crosses her fingers. "Brett and I do have good news that I want to share. You, dear Daddy, will be glad to learn that we finalized the design for our house and we're just waiting for the plans to be approved by the county."

"Good, good, it'll be great to have you close by. I've missed you, kitten. So back to business, your art, I take it?"

"No, not art, it has to do with Stan."

King shakes his head. "Dear Stan, what has he done now?"

"Daddy, you remember how excited Stan was when he learned to ride. He enjoyed it so much that while in Virginia he took lessons at a neighboring stable. The stable was owned by two guys, Andrew Green and Eric Lang. They operate an equine assisted therapy program."

"So what does this have to do with Stan?"

Gabby sits forward. "I think Stan would benefit from that program, but the closest one is outside of Dallas. We need a similar therapy here, don't you agree? I want to start one...for Stan."

"Whoa there, slow down. Let's start at the beginning. What's the name of this thing?"

Gabby reaches across the desk, grabs a cookie and takes a bite before answering. "Equine assisted therapy. It uses horses to help people with injuries regain strength and balance as well as improve their self-esteem. It would be perfect for Stan."

"Have his doctors suggested this, this equine therapy stuff?"

"Since there isn't a program here, I don't believe the doctors know to suggest it. So, I need your help to start one—to help Stan. His accident may leave him with a limp and he has a long recovery ahead of him. He could even help manage the program with his business degree and law degree—it would be perfect. He may need a new job as I don't know if he'll be able to continue working as a mechanic."

"What does Stan think of all of this? Does he want to live here in Texas? Does he want to give up his job? You're making a lot of assumptions here."

"I haven't said anything. I didn't wish to get his hopes up and then you didn't agree and then he would be even more depressed and—"

"So, in that pretty little head of yours, you came up with this idea to help Stan?"

"He's so sad and he—"

"This is just like you, the need to rescue every stray little creature and now this need to help has turned to Stan." King pinches his lips tight and rubs his head.

"We need to help him, Daddy, please."

King remains silent and she searches his face for signs of agreement. What else can she offer to persuade him? "Rita will think you are wonderful."

"Nice try but Rita already thinks I'm wonderful."

"I'll do all the work."

"Gabby, you don't know anything about starting a business."

"You're right, I don't, but I have the smartest daddy in all the world and he knows a lot about business and he'll teach me." She stands behind him and hugs him, then rubs his back. "We'll get to spend time together. Once the election is over, you won't know what to do with yourself. You'll have more time on your hands than you'll know what to do with."

"You're going to be busy with the building of your house. You're spreading yourself pretty thin. Let me think about it."

"Daddy, please, we can hire someone to manage it. Stan can help with that and I can be on the board."

"You really want to do this?"

"It'll help him, and think of all of the other patients just like him—and children, think of the joy it would bring the kids. Instead of rehabilitation in an indoor physical therapy facility, the patients will be outside in the fresh air and excited about learning to ride. They'll smile and forget about their pain. They won't even consider it as therapy."

She leans down and kisses him on the cheek. "This will make me happy."

"All this work will make you happy? It will be work, kitten. No doubt about that."

"Yes, Daddy, please say you'll help. At least look at the proposal. I need your expertise. You're right. I've never done anything like this before."

"Okay, okay, I'll look at it."

"By the way, Andrew and Eric are coming to my engagement party, and I already set up a meeting with the owner of the ranch who runs the veterans program—the one where the vets come and volunteer to take care of the horses. The owner is already on board to expand the facility to include a program that will bring in additional funds, as he is in financial trouble but doesn't want to close. This could be the ideal solution. The vets will still benefit and we can help others like Stan."

"Seems like you already have this in the works. Like I said, I'll look into it. No promises."

She squeals and hugs him. "Thank you. Thank you."

"Mind you, I haven't said yes but I will look at the documents and give you my advice."
She kisses him again.

"I know, Daddy, but you will. It'll be great." She skips out of his office. Her wide smile reminds him of Anna and he reaches for another cookie. How can he say no?

CHAPTER 23

Waco

What happened out there? That's the worst run you've had. What's going on?" Rusty pats Brett on the shoulder. "Talk to me." There is sincerity on the ranch foreman's face reminding Brett that this man cares.

They are at the Waco rodeo for the regional competition. Brett is glad to be away from the crowd and out of the spotlight after finishing his first round. He's dreading having to face King and Gabby and is thankful that Rusty is alone.

He takes off his cowboy hat and shakes his head. "I don't know. Something didn't seem right. I was nervous...unsure of myself." He kicks the dirt with his boot. "I'm sorry. I know everyone is counting on me." He runs his fingers through his curly hair.

"Stop talking like it's over. You could still make the next round, depends on what those other fellows do out there. Your worst is better than some guys' best." Rusty gives a little chuckle. "We'll have to wait it out. No one said this would be easy."

Brett puts his hands on his hips. "Even if I do make it to the next round, if that round goes like this last one, it won't be good."

"I won't argue that, but since we can't change the past, what can we change? If your father could stand here, what advice would Jacob Matthews give you right now, son?"

Brett lowers his head, bites his lip and remains silent. He remembers when he was fourteen years old and competing in the rodeo. Just like today, his first event didn't go as expected. Yes, he remembers the advice his father gave him. He remembers that day well.

"Brett, why do you compete?

"I don't know." Brett hung his head.

Jacob Matthews looked at his son and patted him on the shoulder. "Of course you know. You just lost sight of the reason why you started. Here, take a seat." His father motioned for them to sit on the wooden bleacher that surrounded the arena. "Remember when you roped and tied your first calf? You were about seven years old." The older man's face lit up and he grinned.

"Remember? You were so excited. You jumped around that corral like a bucking bronco gone crazy. I was fixin' to get a horse and rope you just to get you to stop. Then your mama came running out of the house thinking that something bad happened. She was gasping for her breath. Your mama sure did worry." He shakes his head. "In all the excitement, we laughed until the tears rolled down our cheeks. Yes, fond memory, that one."

He paused and stared straight ahead as if watching a movie that was playing in his head before he turned back to face his son. "That's when I knew, I knew you were a chip off the old block. I recognized that energy. Your face told it all because it shone like the sun was blazin' from within. Remember that day?"

"Yes, I remember," Brett said, wondering what this story had to do with the dilemma he currently faced.

"Why do you compete?" his father asked once again. "It's not like school and the law says you gotta go. You chose this path because it spoke to your soul." His father punched his chest with his fist. "In here."

"I do love it," the boy finally acknowledged.

"We're finally getting down to the nitty-gritty." He searched Brett's face. "So, when you were out there today doing what you love, what were you thinkin'?"

"I was nervous, thinking about the points I needed, thinking about John Daniels' tie-down—"

"Whoa, there you have it. The key is focus, focus on you and the calf. That's what got you here. None of that other stuff matters: the arena, the crowd, the other boys, their scores. Nothing matters in that moment but you and that calf." His father patted him on the thigh. "So, let's go and do this thing."

Yes, Brett does remember and his lips curve upward. That day when he was fourteen, he took his father's advice and it worked for him. Focus is the key to being a champion. All that other stuff is extra, making the real task fuzzy.

After remembering his dad's words, he thinks about the small baby who shared the name of this wise man. Brett doesn't know if he'll be the champion today but he does know that he will focus and have fun doing what he loves. He'll do it for his dad. He'll do it for his son.

Gabby's watch vibrates, alerting her that she has been holding her breath. It is an intense few minutes for the entire family as they watch Brett mount Frog, his brown quarter horse, behind the gate in preparation for the few seconds that will determine if all the hard work involved in training and practice can bring success.

Her nerves were put on edge earlier after overhearing bits of a conversation between King and Rusty following the qualifying round in the tie-down competition. The scoreboard answered all questions, showing in the bright neon lights that B. Matthews did not hold first or even second place but was in the middle of the list. However, as long as Brett qualified to continue, that was all that really mattered, and his time and total points were good enough to give him that opportunity. When she kissed him good luck earlier, she could sense his anxiety and she assured him that he would do fine. Out of the corner of her eye she had witnessed her daddy's wink and nod in approval of her efforts to boost Brett's confidence. This was easy to do because she believes in him and she carries enough confidence for both of them.

Now, she gives out a deep yell, jumping up and down and clapping. She doesn't wait for her daddy and Rita. In her haste, she crawls over Stan and his casted leg. Stan had insisted he join the family on this outing and had ignored Rita's warning that the crowd would be too much for him. Since his arm was healed and he was able to use crutches, he eagerly tagged along with the rest of the family.

Gabby runs to complete her quest. She doesn't know what Rusty had said between the rounds but whatever it was, it worked like magic because Brett buckled down and got the job done. She wants to be the first to congratulate him.

Once on the ground floor, she searches and finds Brett tending to Frog in one of the horse stalls under the bleachers. She pushes her way through the circle of fellow competitors.

"Brett, Brett," she yells.

He reaches for her and pulls her through the crowd and lifts her up over his head. She screams with delight. "You did it. I'm so proud of you. We all are."

His grin is wide and his dimple pronounced. "I can hardly believe it."

A reporter thrusts a microphone into Brett's face, pushing Gabby to the side. "How does it feel to win this title?" the young man asks.

"It's amazing." Brett brushes his hair back away from his face, leaving a dirt mark on his forehead.

"Is it true that you are related to the legendary rodeo coach, Jacob Matthews?

"He was my father." Brett looks into the camera.

"From my research you aren't a stranger to the rodeo. You won a similar title about eighteen years ago."

"That's correct."

"You were trained by your father?"

"I sure was."

"Congratulations, Mr. Matthews, on a spectacular run. Thank you for taking the time to speak with us. Folks, let's all give him a well-deserved round of applause."

Gabby hears the noise above her in the arena and catches a

glimpse of Brett on the big screen. She was not aware that they were being televised. A crowd of young rodeo groupies has gathered and the girls want photographs and autographs. She gasps and places her hand on her chest as though trying to catch her sinking heart.

As she allows the others to push her farther away from Brett, some of the nagging insecurities resurface. She felt this a week ago at the tennis club and now she's surprised to be feeling the same way here at the rodeo. She isn't used to sharing or, in this case, taking a back seat. Watching the scene playing out in front of her, she backs away. If Brett complies with all of these requests, he'll be here for a while. When will he notice that she is no longer by his side? She lowers her eyes, turns and leaves.

Rounding the corner away from the horse stalls, underneath the stairs, she hears a familiar voice. Stopping in her tracks, she listens and waits quietly out of sight, turning her back as not to be recognized. She only hears two voices and from the conversation a business deal is going down. Taking in a deep breath, she readies herself for the upcoming unpleasant confrontation.

When the younger man leaves and is out of view, Gabby waits for the second man to emerge from the darkness.

"Stan?"

He jumps as though startled. "Oh, Gabby, it's you."

"What were you doing with that guy?" She motions in the direction the stranger disappeared.

"It's none of your business."

"Really, so that's the way you're going to play this?"

"I don't know what you're talking about."

172

"Stan, I'm surprised. You can do better than that. You're buying drugs."

"Please keep your voice down."

She turns and looks around to make sure they're alone. "What's wrong with you? I don't recognize you anymore." She shakes her head. "I can't believe you're here doing this. You need help. Let me help you. Put that bag into the trash right now." She gestures toward the large can across the way.

"Gabby, it's not what you think?"

"Stan, you're right, it's worse."

When it's clear that he has no intention of parting with his purchase, she walks away, scowling in disgust.

CHAPTER 24

It is late in the evening when the King clan finally sees Waco in their rearview mirror. Brett and Gabby are riding with Rusty and Jamie in the truck pulling the horse trailer, while Stan rides in the car with Rita and King as he requires the entire backseat to support his cast. The two vehicles will caravan until they reach Temple, where they will split; King will continue south to Austin because Stan has a follow-up doctor's appointment in the morning, and Rusty will drive east to the ranch.

In the back seat, Brett enjoys the feel of Gabby snuggled up close with her head on his shoulders. In her lap rests the tie-down champion belt buckle. One would assume that she had been the one who earned it as she hasn't left it out of her sight since the award ceremony. Brett fingers the hard, thick metal that distinguishes this as the real McCoy from the cheap knockoffs that can be bought online.

The King family is proud as Brett accomplished something that none of them could do. All of their wealth and influence could not bring this treasure with its bragging rights back to the ranch. He smiles, reminded of the hard work it took to earn this prize; his afternoons spent lifting weights, running sprints, and the many hours training with Frog so they could perform as a team. He had vowed to win this buckle for his dad and his son. He relaxes his shoulders and leans his head back. If his father were alive, in an unselfish act to express his gratitude for Jacob's expert coaching and mentoring, Brett would have gifted the award to its rightful owner. Brett wonders if little Jacob had sat on his grandfather's knee and watched the rodeo from above.

The ride home has been quiet. Jamie is the first to break the silence. "That was an exciting day, Brett winning and all. And dinner was really good." Still only silence. Jamie turns her head and asks, "You young folks sleeping back there?"

Gabby says with a yawn. "No, Jamie, not sleeping, just tired. It was a busy day."

"I hope Stan will be okay?" Jamie looks out her window.

Gabby lifts her head and sits up straight. "Why do you say that?"

"He didn't seem right, that's all. He was joking when we first got there but as the day went on, he got really quiet. I wonder if his leg was hurting. He didn't complain, though. Rita thought the trip would be too much for him. Maybe his pride kept him from letting his mama know that she was right."

Gabby sits up straight. "He does seem to take a lot of pain pills. Didn't you just get his prescription refilled yesterday?"

"Yes, I did. That's the third time since he's been at the ranch." Jamie turns sideways to face her. "I'm glad he's seeing the doctor tomorrow. One would think that his pain would lessen as time passed. Maybe something isn't healing as it should."

Brett squeezes Gabby's shoulder and encourages her to lean back. All this talk about Stan is annoying. "I'm sure he's fine. You worry too much."

Not distracted by his gesture, Gabby says, "I'm not so sure. He's different from the guy I knew in Washington. His comments are crude to the point of being rude. He swings from appearing happy and jovial one minute to being quiet and moody the next. I'm not a psychiatrist but there's something not right." She wrings her hands.

Brett gives her shoulders another squeeze. "Cut Stan a break. I'm not a fan but he's been through a lot with the accident, and chances are that he'll be left with some sort of disability. I didn't know him before but now he has to deal with the reality that things are different."

"That's kind of you to say." She pats his hand and he flashes his dimple as if to say, *I can be kind to Stan.*

He catches Rusty's stare in the rearview mirror. "I agree that something about that boy is off," Rusty says. "I haven't been able to put my finger on it, but something isn't copacetic."

Gabby draws in her lower lip as she nods her head in agreement. Brett looks out of the window in hopes that this conversation is over. Even though Stan isn't physically present, he is still monopolizing their conversations.

Finally back at the ranch, the night air has a touch of crispness that reminds Gabby fall is right around the corner. She and Brett got a second wind after putting Frog back in his stall, and they want to have an intimate celebration alone.

Standing on the wrap-around porch, she gazes at the stars and makes a wish just like her mother taught her. Her solitude is broken as Brett opens the screen door carrying two glasses of champagne and says, "Just like my beautiful princess ordered." He winks.

Hearing his pet name for her, she smiles, noticing the chiseled bone structure of his face highlighted in the moonlight. She's glad that he's happy; it is well-deserved. Gabby clicks the edge of her flute with his. "Here's to you, Brett Matthews, the best tie-down champion ever!"

"Thank you, fair lady. It does feel good." He wraps his free arm around her waist.

The bubbles from the champagne burst through the liquid surface, teasing her upper lip with an inviting cool moisture.

"You looked so good out there in that final round. Daddy and Rusty are so proud. Rusty's afraid some of the workers will celebrate with all their winnings and they won't show at work tomorrow."

"That so. Doesn't seem right that I'll have to work overtime for winning." He gulps down the last of the champagne. "But let them have their fun. They work hard."

"I'm proud of you too." She leans into his arms and he lifts the glass from her hand, placing it on the table. His lips are eager and she swoons under his touch. After all this time, he still has this effect on her. His touch makes her heart beat a little faster and takes her breath away.

Suddenly he pulls away. "Want to see how fast I can tie you down?"

She giggles. "Sounds interesting." But if she wants to enjoy their time together, she must get something off her chest. It is occupying most of her thoughts. "Hey, can I run something by you?" she says with a serious tone in her voice.

With a puzzled stare, he says, "Sure."

Turning to face the horizon, she begins. "I saw and heard something today at the rodeo that I can't stop thinking about."

There's a pause before she continues. "Stan bought drugs. I don't know what kind or how much. I just know that an exchange was made and from the part of the conversation that I overheard it was some kind of narcotic."

Brett's mouth drops open. "Did I hear you say that Stan bought drugs?"

"Remember how he insisted on coming along today even though Rita strongly advised against it?"

"Drugs...you sure? That's a pretty serious accusation. It doesn't seem like something he would do. He was an attorney before becoming a motorcycle mechanic, right?" Brett scratches his head.

"I'm sure he would get disbarred if he was caught, even though he isn't currently practicing." She rubs her arms as though she is cold. "I think he must hurt more than he lets us believe. The drugs do make sense. He's irritable to the point of being rude. He's downright mean at times. He's not at all the person I knew before the motorcycle accident."

"You saw this drug exchange firsthand?"

"Yes, under the grandstand."

"You're one hundred percent sure?"

"Brett, you sound as though you don't believe me."

He turns her to face him. "I do believe you. I just want you to be absolutely certain. This is serious." She nods and her eyes glisten.

Brett hands her his cell phone and says, "He shouldn't be asleep yet."

"Who...Stan?" She holds the phone at arm's length.

"No, your father. This is serious, too big for you or for me. King will take care of it."

"But, but..." She's at a loss for words.

He lifts her chin to meet his eyes. "Answer one question, will you be able to sleep tonight if you don't make that call?"

"No."

"Well, that settles it." Brett takes back his phone and pushes King's number. After one ring he hands the phone back to her.

"Daddy, we need to talk."

PART IV

CHAPTER 25

Austin

Wiping her forehead, Gabby's eyes follow her artwork hung on the massive wall of The Gallery to the vaulted ceiling towering above. The openness of the modern building allows artwork on this interior wall to be viewed from multiple floors, making the job of hanging a show more complex.

Having complete control over this process reminds her how much she has come to rely on Rita's expertise. Today the task is hers alone, as an employee called out sick and Rita had to manage ArtSmart instead of coming to help her here. *Of all days*, Gabby thinks, swinging her trinity knot back on forth on the chain around her neck.

Closing her eyes, she prays for objectivity, then reopens them, hoping to engage her surroundings as if she's a visitor experiencing this exhibit for the first time. Does this wall have a pleasing composition? Do the adjacent frames complement one another?

Foremost and so basic even for an untrained eye, are the paintings level? Nothing can irritate an audience more, especially people suffering from obsessive compulsive disorder, than to see paintings that hang a bit lopsided.

Taking a seat on the bench in the middle of the gallery, she rolls her head from side to side in an effort to release some tension that has been building in her neck and shoulders. *Enjoy, you have waited two years for the privilege to get your work inside this prestigious gallery. Other artists would gladly take your place right now. This is your dream, embrace it.*

She stares at the three-story wall again. This wall holds the bulk of her work starting on the third floor with her Trinity Knot series, the same paintings that she displayed in January of this year at ArtSmart. The second floor displays her Zeppelin Bend series and the pastel abstracts that she showcased on the East Coast, but this series is new to her Texas audience, and finally here, on the main floor, will be the debut of The Hitch series. The star painting in this series is the one entitled "Forever," the painting that she presented to Brett the night she proposed.

On this section in the gallery she'll also showcase all of the works that she created during her convalescence since the miscarriage. If one were to step back and analyze the groupings of the artwork, one would quickly come to the conclusion that this was a sort of artist's autobiography as the paintings tell the events of her life.

Drawing her attention away from the exhibit, her thoughts move to the present moment. Thinking about Brett and her efforts to move forward makes her lips curve into a smile in anticipation of the wonderful evening when this gallery will be full of her friends, family, and clients as she and Brett formally announce their relationship.

The ringing of her phone breaks her thoughts.

She answers. "Ella, it's so nice to hear your voice. When are you getting into town? I miss you."

"Not until Friday, girlfriend."

"Darn, I was hoping for some girlfriend time before the party."

"Will's been super busy with work and we just can't get away any earlier. Sorry, Gab. Will wanted to visit Stan ever since he heard that he was in rehab. I don't understand how Stan could get into drugs. How's he doing?"

"I haven't seen him this week yet, but Rita says he's coming along. I understand that he's still upset with me for calling him out."

"For what it's worth, Gabby, Will and I both think you did the right thing."

"Thanks for telling me that. Apparently, Stan doesn't."

"The longer it went on, the worse Stan would be. Really, Gab, you did him a favor. He'll come around."

"I hope you're right."

"Hey, I'm looking forward to seeing you but there's something you need to know."

"Oh, is everything all right?"

"Everything's terrific."

"Okay, so what is it?" In the past Ella has always been full of surprises so Gabby's curiosity is getting the best of her.

"You know that I would never want to hurt you, right?

"Ella, just tell me. What's going on? Are you and Will having problems?"

"No, no, nothing like that. In fact, we're great." There's silence and Gabby hears Ella take in a deep breath. "Gabby, I'm pregnant."

Silence again.

Finally, Ella speaks, "Did you hear me? I'm pregnant."

"You're pregnant?" Gabby's tone is flat. "Wow, how far along?"

"Far enough that I have to wear maternity clothes. The baby's due the first week of April." More silence. "Gabby, I thought you should know before the party."

"No, Ella, this is great news," she says, choking back tears. "I'm happy for you."

"You mean that, Gab? I was so worried that you'd be upset. Will thought it was best to wait...wait until you had time to adjust. I was dying here, not being able to share this exciting news with my best friend. It's going to be wonderful...me, a mother."

Did she just say "dying here?" Did she need to use that word? She doesn't know what that word means. Her knees buckle and she sits on the bench and leans forward with her elbows on her knees. It feels as if the air in her lungs was just sucked out of her. However, she manages to speak.

"Me upset, no. Congratulations. Does Rita know?" Her voice quivers.

"She's thrilled. It's her first grandchild. She's already sending packages. Yesterday, the cutest little pink dress came."

"It's a girl?"

"Yes, a precious girl."

"Who else knows?"

"Well, Stan, of course. We thought that the news that his

first niece is on the way would help him to try harder. You know, encourage him to get better."

This hurts, and the pain is more than she can bear. Thinking quickly, Gabby says, "Ella, I'm really sorry but I have to go. The gallery manager is here," she lies.

"Okay, girlfriend, see you Friday. Can't wait."

Still seated, Gabby continues to rest her elbows on her thighs to maintain her balance. Her legs dangle and feel like Jell-O and her chest is tight, making it hard to breathe. *Take a deep breath. You'll be fine.* How did she ever get off the phone before alerting Ella of her true feelings? The news is terribly upsetting, coming as a tremendous blow to an already crippled spirit. She's reminded of one of her mother's favorite sayings whenever a situation seemed unbearable. "This too shall pass." These words were meant to find comfort but that comfort isn't within reach. How long will it take before she'll accept Ella's pregnancy? It isn't in her character to be selfish.

Again, she glances upward to her paintings. The three floors of paintings are a testament of long hours of hard work that represent an outpouring of her soul; some painted with strokes of joy and elation, others painted with a heavy hand guided by sorrow and grief. Now after learning of her best friend's pregnancy, surrounded by her canvases showcased in this grand space, the artist hangs her head. At this moment, if she were a canvas, someone viewing it could easily interpret the despair in the painting. Her canvas would be painted gray with sharp, hard-edged, angry lines that are swallowed into a hole, a vacuum of more gray emptiness. Time stops and she needs to remember to breathe.

Consumed by these feelings of grief and self-pity, it takes Gabby a minute to comprehend that the rhythmic noise is from approaching footsteps. As she turns in the direction of the sound, the glare from the tall front windows disguises his face, but there is only one man who has this particular swagger. *What's he doing here?* She stands, runs her fingers through her hair and wipes the corners of her eyes. The shock of seeing him has forced her to compose her distraught self rather quickly. *Can I take another emotional hit?* She crosses her arms tightly against her body, giving herself a hug for courage.

Richard greets her first with a smile and then an embrace, followed by a light brush of his lips too close to her mouth. His aftershave, accompanied by his gentle touch, reminds her of their shared past when love blossomed. This quick awakening of former passion scares her. For the past few months just a glimpse of him repulsed her. What's wrong with her? *I'm being silly or maybe emotionally exhausted. Since he's Jacob's father, is that the link causing this scary connection?*

Her head is spinning and she's unsure as to what to think or say or do. However, she's sane enough to surmise that she is vulnerable and hurting. If she continues down this path, these peculiar thoughts combined with her distress over Ella's pregnancy would be enough to push her over the edge. Caution will be her motto.

"Richard, this is a surprise." Unable to look at his face, she plays with her folder in an attempt to stall, allowing time to organize her thoughts and still her racing heart.

"I needed a break from the office and was getting some fresh air when I saw your dad and Stan at the new Tex-Mex restaurant on Main Street. I understand that Stan is allowed out on day trips for good behavior. It's good to see him out of a wheelchair, getting around some on his own even if he still needs crutches. Terrible accident he suffered and now the drug thing—awful." He shakes his head. "They mentioned you were here at The Gallery hanging a show."

"I'm glad he's getting the help he needs. We couldn't provide all the treatment he required at the ranch. After some persuasion from Daddy, he agreed to counseling and rehab in town."

"Oh, yes, King can be extremely persuasive." He smiles and gives a knowing nod.

Glad to change topics, Gabby asks, "How's the campaign going?"

"It's going. Polls predict a tight race." He holds his gaze. "Thanks for asking."

Her stomach churns and she bites the inside of her cheek. She needs to get him to focus on something, anything other than stare at her. "So...what do you think?" She raises her hands in the air and pivots three-hundred-sixty degrees.

His eyes follow the works that adorn the gallery walls. Slowly she sees him lift his head to the last floor before he turns his attention back toward her.

"Your style has changed." He pauses. "You've changed."

"How so?" She's intrigued. He has her undivided attention now. "Please explain."

"When we first met, you were so young and innocent, happy and carefree. Everyone was drawn to you. But now, well, you're reserved. It's almost as if you're being overly careful, almost like someone who expects a demon around every corner."

"Maybe I'm not as naïve. Once upon a time and not so long ago, I believed the fantasy that everyone's intentions were for good." She pretends to view her Zeppelin Bend series on the second floor. "That sure was wishful, but flawed, thinking. Some would label my new thinking as a step toward maturity. Besides, we were talking about my art, not me."

"Yes, well, Gabby, honestly, I didn't come here to talk about art. I came here to talk about us, you and me." He reaches for her hands.

She finds it difficult to face him. She's nauseated and her hands are sweating.

"I can make you happy. We were good together. Surely, you have to agree. It wasn't all bad. We can have a great future. Together, there is no end to all we can accomplish: the Senate, the governor's mansion, maybe even the White House. You and me, Gabby, think about it." He squeezes her hands harder. "I need you to do this with me. Your father planned this for us."

She rolls her eyes before turning away as shivers run up her spine. *Are we really having this conversation now? I have to accept that my best friend is going to be a mother, reminding me that she'll have the precious baby I lost, and now this. How dare he use my daddy in his argument? Life is throwing me one punch after another—TKO, total knockout. Careful, girl.*

"You look confused. It isn't that hard. It's quite simple really. Listen to me. We had a bad patch. All relationships have highs and lows—you learn from them and grow. I wasn't perfect and I'm not promising you I'll be perfect in the future, but to throw away everything, our incredible future and for what?" He lets go of her hands and throws his up in the air.

"For him, some tennis playboy or cowboy or whatever he's pretending to be these days. You can't be serious about this engagement. You had a fling, you wanted some fun, to let loose.

You wanted to get back at me, hurt me, give me a taste of my own medicine. I got it, Gabby. You made your point but this craziness has got to stop. You're making a fool out of yourself. Everyone can see it. Well, everyone except you."

She turns to face him again and bites her lip, wondering if he can read the fury in her eyes. She shakes her head.

"What kind of a life can you have with him?" He reaches for her hands again. "I can give you the life you deserve. Please, Gabby, you're not thinking clearly. Let this childish behavior go."

She pulls her hands away. "I love him." Her voice is firm.

"You loved me once, remember?" She looks away so she cannot see him wearing the pitiful look that would match his words. "You could love me again. I've changed. Give me a chance. I miss us." He brushes back a stray strand of her hair and turns her chin so their eyes meet.

"I tried to go on without you and give you time to come to your senses. You're confused. Anyone would be after everything that you've been through. I know you felt obligated with the baby, but you don't have to marry him. It isn't love that you feel." He raises his arms up in the arm in the victory sign. "You're free."

"It wasn't his baby." She surprises herself that the words come out so quickly. Her deep hidden secret is exposed. Without giving it a second thought, she has revealed the truth. Wow, she didn't intend for that to happen!

"What?" He wrinkles his brow and his eyes dart back and forth across her face.

"It wasn't Brett's baby. It was yours. You were the father." She reads the shock on his face. His mouth drops open and he runs his fingers through his hair.

"Why didn't you tell me?"

She takes a deep breath in an attempt to appear strong. "It would have complicated matters." He looks at her as if he doesn't understand.

"We broke up. You're running for office. The press would have been all over it, investigating everything from your infidelity, and lord only knows how many women would surface, to your little scrape with the law. It would have been ugly and not the kind of publicity that a candidate wants. But, like you said, it doesn't matter anymore." She lowers her head and fights back the tears.

He takes her hand once more. "I'm not the press, Gabby. You should have told me. I had a right to know. I would have been there for you and for our baby."

"I know. I'm sorry." Her voice is weak, trembling, and her lower lip quivers. "I wanted to tell you. At first, I didn't tell anyone, not even Brett. I left town and was trying to figure out what was best for the baby."

He wraps her in his arms to stop her from shaking. Inwardly, she blames herself for not being strong enough to hide her emotions.

"I'm so sorry our baby died." This sentiment causes her to collapse deeper into his arms. "I really want to be angry with you. You know that, right?" He holds on tight and brushes the top of her hair with his cheek. "Wow, our baby."

"Please don't," she sniffles. Her eyes overflow and the salty liquid spills over and follows down her face to the corners of her mouth.

"I love you, Gabby. I couldn't live with myself if I neglected to tell you how I feel. I want to work this out. Give us another chance. We'll make more babies, you'll see."

Pulling away from him, she wipes her eyes. The black mascara smudged on her fingers is a sign that she must look a mess.

"We belong together. Please..." He turns her face and she stares into his pleading eyes. His earnestness seems almost real. A year ago she would have believed him; however, she's determined not to fall into his trap.

"If you were honest with yourself, you would see that I wasn't enough for you," she says with firmness "When we were together, you were still searching for something or someone that I wasn't. Your someone is out there—you just haven't found her yet but I'm sure it isn't me because my someone is Brett. We love each other. It's something that I can't explain. We just know that we're meant to be together. You and I are over, Richard. We've been over for a while now. It's time to move forward."

"You make it sound so easy." He looks at his feet.

"When it's real, it is easy. What Brett and I share is the real deal. Are you still seeing...what's her name...Amanda? She's very pretty."

He looks at her with surprise. "She's a model. She's not you. She looks good on my arm and when we walk into a room, I know all heads are turning because of her, not me. She seems to like all the attention this campaign stuff brings and, truth be told, she knows the schedule better than I do. I'm not sure if it's me she's attracted to or all the attention she gets when she's with me." Richard squeezes her shoulders.

"You and I for what it's worth, we really did make a great couple." He draws her close to him again. "I'll always be there for you."

She backs away, not wishing to get drawn in to his embrace. "Friends," she says, reaching out her hand.

"Friends?" he asks as if in disbelief. "That's all you can give me? Can you at least consider it, consider us?"

"We're over. I've moved on. You need to do the same." Her strong voice comes as a surprise.

"That will take some getting used to." Clearly annoyed, he puts his hands in his pockets and shuffles his feet, but he stops pressing the issue. He looks around the gallery as if defeat is hard for him to accept.

After a few awkward seconds, Gabby asks, "Are you coming to the reception?"

Richard gives a small chuckle. "Do you think your daddy would miss an opportunity for exposure? Sorry to be taking some of the limelight but it can't be helped. With the campaign so tight, I need all the publicity I can get. Look at it this way, you'll benefit as your art will be mentioned on the front pages."

"Richard, you're going to do great things. You'll be a fine senator."

"Thanks for the vote of confidence. Some days, I'm not so sure."

"I'm glad we had this conversation before the party. I feel better getting everything out in the open." She looks up at him. "Bring Amanda to the party. I'll introduce her to some of my old sorority sisters." He smiles down at her and takes her hand.

"That's very thoughtful, but that's how you are, always thinking of others."

He steps away and looks down at his watch. "I better go. I'm late." He brushes her cheek with a light kiss before walking toward the exit. After a few steps, he stops and turns. "By the way, I do like your work. Much like you, it's matured over the years, more complex like an old-world wine."

"Thanks, Richard," she calls after him.

Again he stops and turns. "For what?"

"For understanding." She wrings her hands. This time he nods before turning. She watches and listens to the rhythmic sound of his shoes on the marble floor, until he is out of sight.

She covers her face with her hands for a moment. Then after grabbing her blond hair with both fists, she raises her eyes to the heaven and opens her arms in a big stretch. She sighs in relief that the cage hiding her secret has been unlocked.

Her soul should be free, but it is still tormented, first by the weight of Ella's pregnancy pulling her down, now combined with this unexpected exchange with Richard. She fumbles through her purse. When Doctor Stevens handed her the card in the hospital, she never intended to have a need. Now, with nervous fingers she dials the number. Dealing with a constantly fluctuating barrage of emotions has taken a toll, wearing her down; she is tired of putting up a good front. How can she manage? Is she too fragile or is this too big? *I need help.*

CHAPTER 26

Gabby steps into the sunlight; however, the glare isn't blinding as she donned her Oakleys to hide her red, swollen eyes before leaving the psychiatrist's office, which is located in the heart of the commercial district above busy high-end store fronts. Perhaps treating herself to a shopping spree will make her feel better. It will be a reward for being brave enough to make the appointment that caused her to pour out her pain to a stranger. It took courage, along with swallowing a great deal of pride, to acknowledge the humbling realization that she wasn't strong enough to handle the events life had thrown her way.

She looks up and down the street: Gucci, Prada, Chanel. Where should she begin? She'll buy a different style dress, maybe the newest trend. Before making a decision, she digs into her purse to retrieve her cell phone. If she wants to distance herself from her past, now is the time to start before her newly acquired strength dissipates. She dials the number of the contractor and leaves him a voicemail asking him for an update because she wishes the house for her and Brett to be completed as soon as possible.

After hanging up, she pulls back her shoulders with pride. Minutes after leaving the office, she has made progress and happily will have something new to report in the session tomorrow, since the doctor strongly encouraged her to have daily sessions this week. This requires her to stay in town and away from Brett. She could use her show as an excuse. On second thought, keeping secrets has caused trouble, and Brett already warned her about not confiding in him. She remembers how she hid her pregnancy and how she couldn't bring herself to tell him that Stan would be convalescing at the ranch. Recalling arguments, she hangs her head in shame. Brett deserves better.

She's made mistakes; doesn't everyone? But hasn't she learned from them? Isn't she wiser? Yes, she'll confide in Brett. She'll tell him about the psychiatrist and she will tell him about Ella's pregnancy and how it makes her feel sad. However, she isn't going to tell him about her talk with Richard. She's sure that Brett will get his guard up and confront Richard. A showdown between the two men at the reception would certainly make the front page, but it wouldn't be the publicity her daddy is hoping to achieve by inviting the press to her party. She loves Brett and he loves her, but that doesn't mean they have to share everything, right?

Adjusting her bag's shoulder strap, she heads toward Gucci. The racks are full of fall fashions but nothing tempts her, and she exits without a trip to the dressing room. Meandering down the sidewalk, her eyes are lured by something bright and shiny. She holds her head high and walks through the revolving door of the jewelry store.

After her inquiry, the salesman hands her the watch. The wide steel band seems strong and durable and there is a single quarter-carat diamond set into every third link, while the face of the watch also has diamonds marking the quarter hour. The watch sure is trendy and it will be the perfect gift. Knowing the purchase will exceed the limit of her MasterCard, without hesitating she pulls out her daddy's bank card. King insisted she carry it for a rainy day, and with all the tears she's shed, today certainly qualifies. The rain gauge is overflowing.

"Would you like this gift-wrapped?" the clerk asks.

"Yes, please." She smiles at the salesman. He probably thinks her pleased with the purchase but he's only half right. She's thinking about rainbows. Her storm was passing, no more thunder, no more rain—instead, a rainbow is gracing her sky, and sometimes even a rainbow needs some encouragement.

CHAPTER 27

Gabby sits on an upholstered chair near the window overlooking a small garden that gives the patients a respite from the gray walls of the institution. The rehabilitation center is on the east side of town. A cardboard tray holding two steaming cups of coffee occupies the table. She usually doesn't drink coffee in the afternoon, but in efforts of reaching a truce, she's making an exception. Her foot swings as she fills the time by checking messages on her phone.

The metal latch clicks as an older woman, clearly a volunteer, opens the modern glass door allowing Stan's large frame, complete with crutches, to enter. His leg sports a smaller cast and he seems to maneuver without difficulty. When he comes near, she rises and brushes his cheek with her own. He stands firm with his eyes fixed forward. Aware that he's avoiding eye contact, she smiles anyway.

"I brought us coffee. It's hot."

Continuing to act as if he's absorbed in watching something beyond the window, he asks, "To what do I owe this occasion, this visit from a snitch? Betrayal hurts."

"Please, Stan, refer to me as your stepsister, someone who cares for you." She wrings her hands. "I'm sorry you feel that I betrayed you."

"I have a right to be angry."

"I was worried and you needed help."

"You could have quenched your desire by coming to me, instead of involving your father and my mother." He still looks straight ahead. She tugs at his sleeve.

Suddenly, he shakes his head. "Guess I can't stay angry forever. Coffee in this place sucks. Shame to let this get cold." He nods toward the cups. His eyes finally find hers before lowers his body into the chair.

"Here, let me get the stool to prop up your leg." She pushes the hassock in front of his leg and he swings his cast up on it.

"Which one is mine?"

She happily hands him the coffee. "Black and robust, just the way you like it."

He takes a sip and closes his eyes. "Heavenly."

She smiles at him again and picks up her latte. "How are you?"

"They tell me I'm making great improvements. I'm looking forward to my discharge. I miss French food." He chuckles.

She sits forward in her chair. "How is your pain? Are they able to get it under control?"

"Pain is still there. Better though. In lieu of additional medication, I'm learning distraction techniques: relaxation therapy, music, meditation, you know, stuff like that." He touches her hand. "You're a distraction."

This time she is the one to look away as she can feel the heat in her face. "Do you need anything?"

"Other than getting the hell out of here?" He takes another sip of coffee. "I need to be normal—get this cast off, walk, ride my bike and not have to deal with the pain."

"I can relate to the pain. We have something in common." He tilts his head as if begging to hear more.

"The pain here in my heart." She touches her chest. "The pain makes it hard for me to breathe. I feel this incredible sadness. I try to paint to express the grief and the loss, but it's not enough. I still hurt, but I went around painting a happy face in order to fool everyone—but the pain never leaves. It lingers on and I got tired, really tired." A tear rolls down her cheek. She doesn't bother to wipe it away. "So I started seeing a psychiatrist. It is helping."

"I had no idea. I'm sorry, Gabby." He reaches for her hand once more and squeezes tight. "I was so wrapped up in my own pain that I didn't notice yours."

"It's not your fault. I hid it under the disguise of busyness, so my therapist says."

He pats her hand. "I'm glad you're seeing someone. I found that talking about it helps."

"We're quite the pair, aren't we?" She sniffles and laughs.

Then he laughs with her. "Yes, we are."

"They say that time has a way of healing. The bad seems to have less significance after it is faced and understood."

He nods. "Your party is only a few days away. If you need more time you can always cancel. Your friends and family will understand."

She wrinkles her brow. "I don't want to cancel. I need to make positive experiences." She sits up straight in her chair. "I hung my show on Monday. The gallery is a beautiful venue. It feels good to be working again. Like you said, getting back to normal is good. Are you coming to the party?"

Stan clears his throat. "They do allow me passes since I checked myself in voluntarily. But I'm not sure that I'm ready to see people. Besides, it may not be good for my rehab, nor my heart for that matter." His words accompanied by his stare forces her to turn away. She bites her lip.

"So you're still going through with it?"

"The reception...of course, I waited two years to have a show there."

He shakes his head quickly. "No, the engagement."

"Stan, I love Brett and, yes, we're getting married."

"Have you talked this over with your psychiatrist?"

"Really, Stan? I don't need a psychiatrist to tell me that Brett is the best thing that ever happened to me. But to answer your question, yes, she agrees that moving forward is the best way to put the past into perspective. I'm moving forward with Brett by my side."

He hangs his head.

"Please, be happy for me. Be happy for us." Stan continues to look at his cast. She changes the subject.

"Will and Ella arrive at the end of the week. I'm looking forward to seeing them."

At that, Stan raises his head. "Yes, they're coming here straight from the airport. They'll brighten my day. Ella's preg—" He stops speaking.

"You can say it, Ella's pregnant. She told me earlier this week."

Be calm and still relaxed. Am I hiding my feelings or can he see right through me? "It seems I'm the last person to find out the news."

"She was giving you time."

Gabby looks at her lap and picks at her fingernails. "I know. It hurts realizing that you seem so fragile that everyone walks on eggshells. I hate that." Stan nods as if in agreement.

Gabby says, "Ella's pregnancy has been a major topic in my therapy sessions."

"You're the major topic in my sessions."

"Stan, don't."

"I know. I know. You don't want folks to walk on eggshells around you so I'm not. I'm being open and totally honest; making myself vulnerable." He searches her face before adding, "Do you know how hard I have tried to forget you? I was thinking about us when I crashed." He reaches for her hand and she allows it.

"When I'm on my bike, I'm free. It takes concentration to ride fast and hard so that there is no space to think of anything else. This ride, my accident, you were such a strong presence I couldn't get you out of my thoughts even when it meant my life. I don't think you understand."

She bites her lip and allows him to continue.

"I've been riding for years and I prided myself on my expertise. I know that I can't have you. When I saw the way you looked at him that night this summer at the gallery in Virginia, I knew. But knowing something in your mind and knowing in your heart are two entirely different things." He stares off into the distance.

She feels his sadness and an outpouring of compassion runs

through her veins. This is the Stan that she first knew. The old Stan is back, but how can she help him? Sadly, she can't.

"It will just take time. Thanks for sharing. This can't be easy for you. I never meant to hurt you," she says. "Brett and I have had some difficult times but our love has survived. He makes me happy. There's something between us that I can't explain. It's special and somewhere out there, there is a special girl waiting for you. You're a great guy. It will happen."

"I hope you're right—first Will and Ella got together and now you and Brett."

She gives his hand a firm squeeze. "Sounds like you should start moving forward as well. When you find your special someone, you'll forget all about me."

"In due time, but now I need to focus on walking. This cast comes off next week. That's when the real therapy will start. I'm anxious to get started. Sitting around in this cast for the past six weeks has been one of the hardest things I've ever done."

"I'm your friend, Stan, and Brett could be your friend. Daddy would like for all of us to get along."

He sighs. "Too early for that. Just seeing the two of you together makes my blood boil."

She feels the need to defend Brett. "You would like him if you gave him a chance." She looks up so she can peer into his brown eyes. "Stan, I'm glad you're part of our family. Promise me that if you need anything that you will call me."

"Thanks, Gabby." He checks out his watch and follows it with a huge gulp of coffee. "Thanks for stopping by and thanks for the coffee. Time for PT." He uses his crutches to stand. "I'm glad you came by."

"Me too," she says as she stands and watches him until he is out of sight.

Even though she yearns to take away his genuine sadness, it's obvious that therapy is helping since he seems like the kind and sensible guy that she knew before.

There is a swing in her step as she leaves the rehabilitation center and checks the mental box marked *Resolve the conflict with Stan.* She feels happier than she has felt in months and she is excited to report her progress at her afternoon session. Perhaps therapy is helping her as well.

Gabby finds a parking space along the main street and enjoys the sun on her face as she walks the few blocks to the psychiatrist's office. As she pauses to check the menu outside the new, chic tapas restaurant, her cell phone rings.

"Hey, beautiful."

"Brett, this is a nice surprise. How are you feeling? I didn't call you this morning after hearing about your late-night party. I thought you should sleep in. How's the hangover?"

"Oh, we must have a rat."

"Oh, sweetie, don't be harsh. There is no need to call Daddy names. I'm glad you had fun."

"It was fun last night but now I'm eating crackers and Tylenol with my coffee."

She smiles and in a teasing tone she says, "Here I am working hard hanging my show and tending to all of these last-minute details for our special night and you are out partying."

"The guys were fun. It was good of them to want to celebrate my win. They kept buying me shots and I didn't know how to refuse. I hope I didn't embarrass myself."

She can't imagine Brett out of control.

"Hey, the reason I called—a package arrived today."

"Oh, really?"

"It's quite a gift, very expensive. No card, though. I must have a secret admirer."

She beams as he seems pleased. "Really? Who do you think sent it?"

"Maybe the Fed Ex man made a mistake and it should have gone across the street to that real good-looking neighbor. The one you think is sexy."

"Could it possibly be from someone who wants to spend the rest of time with you?"

"The rest of time, you say?"

"Yes, the reason for the watch."

"I never told you it was a watch but very clever of you. I'm glad you explained."

She is anxious and the question quickly pops out, "But do you like it?"

"Like it. I love it."

Is that joy that she hears in his voice? She had hopes of appreciation so joy is a bonus.

"Gabby, you shouldn't have."

"Stop that. I love you and this is my gift to start our future together. I'm glad you love it. You can thank me later." She giggles.

"How about tonight? I was hoping you would be coming back to the ranch. We could have a picnic by the lake."

"I'd like to but—"

"But what? I miss you, princess. Your show is hung and the party is still a few days away. Please."

"You're so cute when you beg, but I really can't. I'm sorry." She hears only silence. "Brett, I'm in therapy." Still there is no response. "I've been unable to shake this grief, and Doctor Stevens had referred me to a psychiatrist. I've been having appointments daily and I know that it's helping." She rubs her forehead. "I miss you too and I'm sorry. I haven't been fair to you lately. I'm moody and sad and—"

"Hey, I understand. Really, I do. I miss you but you haven't been yourself lately. I struggle not knowing the right thing to say. The doctor said it would take time, but if you think this therapy is helping then I'm all for it. Anything to get things back to how they used to be."

She twirls a few strands of blond hair around her finger. "Thanks for understanding. I really do miss you."

"You'd better."

After the call is disconnected, Gabby stands straighter. Matching the sun's rays warming her arms and face, she also feels a warm light penetrating the cold darkness that has been lurking within, attempting to steal her joy. This warmth is making her stronger and she lifts her eyes giving thanks for the lessons she has learned.

Everything is so much clearer now. First, she's learned that asking for help doesn't imply weakness but is a sign of wisdom.

Second, she's learned that Brett is on her side and she can lean on him. Together they make a team, a partnership based on love and trust. This concept is new and exciting. Why has it taken her so long to realize something that now seems obvious?

While still admiring the crystal-clear blue sky, she smiles. The glow radiates from within and shines on her face as she thinks about sharing a life together with Brett. She loves this man more and more as time goes by.

CHAPTER 28

In her condo later that evening, Gabby brushes whimsical strokes on the giant canvas. She has no concrete plan but has started with a horizontal composition, using azure blue for a sky and fern green for the ground. She'll practice some techniques from an article she saw in one of her monthly art magazines. Stepping away from the canvas, holding her brush in the air, her eyes glow as she examines her creation. Feelings of joy and happiness seem to leap out of her chest. Proud of this accomplishment, she pauses to review a mental checklist of her life.

All in all, she's giving her therapy an A+. The first appointment was tough but with each session thereafter it became easier to unburden her soul. It has also been rewarding that the psychiatrist seems genuinely pleased with her progress. Now Gabby views herself as the model patient since she resolved her conflict with Stan, revealed to Richard that he was her baby's father, and affirmed her commitment to Brett by building the house by the lake.

The biggest benefit to therapy, however, was that it allowed her to voice her thoughts about Ella's pregnancy. She hasn't totally resolved her conflicting feelings about that, but she is in a much better place than when she first heard the news. Therapy has been mentally and emotionally draining, but she's able to breathe deeper, feeling a sense of accomplishment for having the courage to go through it.

Closing her eyes, her imagination is all-encompassing as she visualizes the art reception combination engagement party.

He'll look handsome in his black tuxedo. All will take notice of his physique as he strides across the room, flashing a dazzling smile accentuating his dimple. She remembers very clearly the last time she saw Brett in a tuxedo. It was Valentine's Day, just six months ago, that she and Brett shared that first dance. They were at the Valentine's Ball sponsored by the country club. Brett, the club's dashing unattached tennis pro, had women lined up around the dance floor waiting for their turn for him to swirl them around the dance floor. At the time Gabby had thought the women foolish, but at the same time she was surprised at the twinge of jealousy she experienced when Ella expressed her desire to dance with Brett.

Now, all of her memories seem like a different lifetime as so much has happened since that evening. Gabby closes her eyes and continues with her memory.

Richard had arrived late, reeking of his secretary's perfume. It wasn't the first time he had cheated. He had begged forgiveness and swore that it would never happen again, but Gabby didn't stick around to see if he was able to keep his word, for she ended their relationship. It hurt her that Richard chose to parade his indiscretion on the day that lovers all over the world recommit to their relationships and whisper, "I love you." Could this be the reason she was so decisive to end the relationship?

However, it was later on that very night that she had dropped her guard and allowed Brett to get close enough to work his charm. She was never a woman who had one-night stands, and with Brett's reputation as a playboy, she knew that she was playing with fire. Her anger had made her open to his advances and she had fallen for him just like all the others. She tried to push him away but when he kissed her, their chemistry was like magic.

Now, she takes in a deep breath and the memory is clear. She allows her thoughts to take her back when she first responded to love's call to dance.

It was that February evening. Aware that someone had joined her on the porch, she detected his musky scent long before she saw him. When he approached, he trapped her by placing his arms on the railings on either side. Her heart raced and when he touched her arm it was as if electricity pulsed through her, causing her lip to quiver uncontrollably. And that was when he turned her around and she longed to find her reflection in his emerald eyes. As they danced, he serenaded her with gentle low tones that whispered of love, and his breath tickled her ear. She had difficulty standing, as if he were a drug intoxicating her, and she leaned into his muscular frame. When his lips touched hers, the chemistry was magical but scary. No kiss or touch before had ever sneaked into her soul. Why did this man move her so?

Yes, she remembers it as if it was yesterday, and soon the world will know that Brett is pledged to her and her alone.

Returning to her canvas, she paints with quick, purposeful

strokes. Her energy is transferred from her hand through the brush. Thick horizontal strokes of paint give the impression of fields, swirls of green indicate dancing trees, and scattered dabs of yellow and pink suggest flowers. The scene before her is a paradise and sparks an idea.

Her eyes are wide and she squeals with excitement. Yes, she can create her own paradise—and it can start the night of the reception. Glancing at her watch, she sees it is after one a.m.

PART V

CHAPTER 29

I n an effort to calm her nerves, Gabby watches a cardinal perched on the branch of the old oak outside the window of her condo. Usually viewing nature relaxes her but today it isn't working. She's jittery and can't seem to concentrate. She's always experienced some degree of anxiety before every reception, but today her level of anxiety is at an unusual peak. When first planned, this engagement party was to be simple but now it has turned into something much more.

Earlier this morning as if on cue, pink roses arrived at her doorstep. Her daddy has always sent them for every opening reception. She tried calling him but her words of thanks went to his voicemail. Disappointed, she bites her lower lip; she'll shower him with appreciation when they meet later today.

She breathes in the sweet smell of the roses and enjoys the touch of the delicate petals against her cheek, though not even these beautiful flowers can settle the anxiety that is percolating in her gut. As she taps her fingernails on the rim of her Van Gogh "Starry Night" mug, she stops to admire her grandmother's ring, noticing its brilliance has dulled. A cleaning will be in order before the party this evening. It won't be an imposition since the jewelry store is near her therapist's office. She adds the errand to her to-do list, and then chews on the end of the pen. She had seriously considered canceling her session today with the psychiatrist, but somehow that seemed phony since she told Brett that therapy was the reason that she didn't go back to the ranch earlier this week to spend some time with him.

Since she's still checking her watch every minute, it's obvious that watching the birds out the window isn't working. What should she do next to quiet the butterflies in her stomach? She tries using a few of the meditation exercises she learned, but after the first few seconds of her deep breathing exercises, the sound of her cell causes her to jump several inches off her chair.

"Miss King, we're here at the ranch but we need someone to open the gate. I tried the call box but no one answers."

Recognizing the head contractor's voice, she says, "Oh, Mr. Green, I'm sorry. I can open it." She dials the home number for the ranch and plugs in the code for the gate. She's glad for modern technology that allows her to perform this simple task remotely. Where is everyone, she wonders? After opening the gate, Gabby marvels at the news that the foundation will be under way and, if the weather holds, the house will be finished in six months.

Forgoing any further attempt at meditation, she takes another sip of her morning brew and she concludes that if no one at the ranch answered the callbox, it probably means that the family was already headed to the city. It seems early but perhaps they share in her excitement, and it gives Gabby hope of spending some precious alone time with Brett before the reception.

Glancing out the window again, she shares the joy the cardinal must feel as he chirps and flits from branch to branch as if dancing.

Yes, this evening she and Brett will share a dance. Thinking of announcing their relationship to the public brings to mind Richard's warning about sharing the limelight. She understands politics, and she understands her daddy's desire to capitalize on her reception by hiring reporters to give Richard much needed exposure. With the election only a month away and the polls showing a tight two-party race, stepping up publicity was the right thing to do. But will Richard's presence stress Brett?

Even though the two men share a mutual dislike for each other, surely her talk with Richard earlier this week should help facilitate a peaceful evening. However, she'll do her part to keep distance between them, plus she has confidence that her daddy will ensure that her night will be perfect.

Tonight is going to be their night; so what if Richard is outside the gallery campaigning. She shakes her head as if flinging away bad thoughts. She's overthinking this whole situation. Tonight will be the most incredible night of her life.

CHAPTER 30

Earlier that day

Hﾠigh on a ridge near the northern slope of the King ranch, Brett sits tall in the saddle and surveys the land rolling for miles in the distance. Nearly a dozen cattle are missing from the herd that was moved earlier this week to graze in the lower pasture in preparation for the winter months ahead. It's a mystery, but the dense fog that settled in halfway through the cattle drive is being blamed.

He wishes to please King and has made it his mission to recover the lost cattle. Rusty had instructed the workers to let it wait until Monday, but Brett had heard a rumor that a pack of coyotes was roaming in the area and killing for sport. Last evening one of the wranglers at the adjacent ranch found more than six cattle slain. A coyote pack was last sighted traveling west, but it was possible for them to retrace their tracks and come east or perhaps there was more than one pack. Efforts were made by the government this spring to round up the coyotes, as their numbers had increased greatly with the building of new subdivisions taking the coyotes' hunting ground.

The bulk of the King cattle herd is now safe in the lower pasture as the wranglers are taking turns guarding with the help of dogs to alert them of intruders, but these stragglers lost north of there could very well be in danger and Brett isn't about to let that happen.

Glancing at his new watch, he's aware that he will have to manage his time. Tonight is an important night and Gabby will be furious if he's late. He has only been witness to her losing her temper once—but King warned him that she was slow to anger but when she did get mad it was similar to a volcano violently erupting. He certainly doesn't want to face that.

At breakfast he reassured Rusty and Jamie that he would be leaving for Austin following close behind them, but he lied. As soon as he saw Rusty's truck disappear down the lane, he set out on horseback to find those cattle. He told himself that the task would only take a few hours and then he'd have plenty of time to drive to the city before the evening festivities.

Where are those cattle? He tightens the reins and takes great care to scan the land with his binoculars. Here in the north part of the ranch, the landscape is so rugged that cattle might easily be mistaken for rocks or hidden from view in the overgrowth of grasses. This time of year, the grasses are taller and turning golden brown, making it harder to see cattle grazing among them. He is determined in his mission, though, and is certain of its success.

CHAPTER 31

At the King Ranch

Later that same morning, feeling fortunate that the gate leading into the King ranch is open, Stan instructs the Uber driver to drive down the lane at a slow, steady pace. After tipping the driver, he repositions his backpack and adjusts his crutches, balancing the handles of the large, bulky shopping bag on his forearm as he strides up the ramp leading to the ranch house's front door.

Taking a moment, he surveys the surroundings. All of the vehicles usually parked between the house and the barn are gone except for Brett's Audi. He surmises that Brett must have grabbed a ride with Rusty. With caution he unlocks the front door.

"Hello." Holding his breath, he scans the room. The ticking of the grandfather clock is the only sound, and he exhales in relief as he continues through the door and places his parcel and backpack on the dining room table.

His plan was successful and required him to tell just one itty-bitty lie to obtain his freedom. He secured a proper pass from the rehabilitation center but he failed to disclose that he never intended to return before the ten p.m. curfew. To mislead the nurses, he purposely mentioned that he would be attending the art reception and engagement party, so they'll wait before reporting him, thinking he's out having a grand time and that he's just tardy. It seemed easiest to leave this way, without heated words or calls alerting the doctors, and certainly not allowing time for them to try and get his off-campus privileges revoked. For the first time in a long time, he can lift his head and feels a sense of pride for a mission accomplished.

Earlier today after their plane landed, Will and Ella had stopped by the rehab facility as promised. At first, he thoroughly enjoyed the visit and the opportunity to catch up on everything that was happening in the D.C. area. When they spoke of the future arrival of their baby, though, they seemed so happy that afterwards his loneliness magnified. Yes, he could have tapped into his new repertoire of acquired skills—the meditation, the music and relaxation therapy, or scheduled an impromptu "emergency" counseling session that most likely would have been with a staff member who was nearly half his age and proudly carried a Psych 101 textbook. He kindly passed.

He steps farther into the dimly lit room. Somehow with the absence of the familiar noises and smells from the kitchen, the house seems cold and forgotten, mimicking his mood. Yes, he is melancholy. A sentence he read in a book years before creeps into his mind, reminding him about how painful it is to love someone and not be able to share in her life. This author, Willa Cather, she understood.

He hangs his head because the source of his ailment is obvious.

He doesn't need a shrink. He's not crazy and he's certainly not a drug addict. He sat in that rehab center and skirted the truth for weeks. He fooled them, those white coats with the framed diplomas decorating their offices. He told them what they wanted to hear. He blamed all of his problems on the accident. He purposely avoided mentioning the reason for the distraction that caused the accident. It was similar to a doctor who treats a patient's symptom without looking for the cause.

He is a man desperately in love with a woman who doesn't return his affection and never will, as she loves another. It is so simple but it still sucks. All the therapy in the world isn't going to help. His accident gave him an excuse to build a wall, attempting self-preservation by using his physical pain to medicate his tormented soul. His anger passed; however, anger's companions, depression and bitterness, still hang around.

Using his crutches, Stan pivots to face the large front window and peers out over the vast expanse of land. For him the open space resonates as loneliness, and with that his thoughts go to her. *How lovely she'll look tonight.* He closes his eyes and, like a vivid dream, he imagines it all.

Her hair is up off her shoulders with a few loose curls at the nape of her neck and they lightly brush his face as he takes her into his arms. Their bodies fit together effortlessly. He smells her tantalizing Chanel perfume. He stays here in this moment and a smile rests on his face but then his dream turns into a nightmare. *She stands with Brett at her side.* Stan's eyes pop open and his fist slams into his open hand. Then he runs his fingers through his hair and hangs his head. *God, what does she see in him? Why can't she love me?* After releasing the tension with his outburst, the incredible sadness washes back over him.

Now is not the time for self-pity, however, and try with all his might, he cannot stay angry with her. In hindsight, should he have stayed in town, sucked up his pride, pulled back his shoulders and stood with his family congratulating the couple on the evening of their engagement announcement? No, he isn't ready for that. The wound hasn't healed; it's still fresh and weeping.

Backing away from the window and returning to the dining room, he opens the parcel. Inside is the latest model of a quadcopter, a drone complete with high-definition camera. Unlike the previous models, this one boasts new stabilization technology as well as an improved hover function to allow for smooth video footage. It even has a homing device that senses when the battery is running low, and it would return automatically. He's anxious to operate this new toy and the ranch is the perfect playground.

Stan had owned two drones previously and he learned some expensive lessons. The first model he flew into the side of his condo building, causing the battery pack along with the holding rack to break off. That night with a flashlight, he searched the bushes for nearly two hours without success. The neighbor's dog kept barking from the balcony above creating such a ruckus that he was forced to abandon the mission.

The second drone he flew for three months until the day he took it to the park and managed to get it caught in the top branch of a large oak tree. He worked the controls until the battery went dead and then, short of a gust of wind, his only hope would be for a curious squirrel to give it a push. He reported the mishap to the rangers but nothing ever came of it.

So here he is, out of the rehab center and while the others are attending the party, he will try to restore his charred reputation by becoming a valuable member of this family. His goal is to show King that he is not a liability but an asset. He will prove that he's on par with Brett. He may not be a rodeo champion but he's competent and capable. He'll find those lost cattle.

King had mentioned the missing cattle several times during their lunch together downtown earlier this week when Stan used his day pass to leave the rehabilitation center. That's when Stan made his plan to purchase the drone and outwit Brett and the other ranch hands. If successful, he'll be sure to win back King's respect.

The day is perfect, full of sun and absent of wind. He knows the route as he had plenty of time this past week to study the maps, including the topography. The biggest problem he anticipated would be the loss of cell phone service as in the past, coverage was spotty, but recently a new tower was installed on the outer edge of the northern border of the ranch and Rusty has reported the service improved.

In addition to the map, drone and cellphone, he'll take a backpack with some provisions. The saying "once an Eagle Scout, always an Eagle Scout" comes to mind. With everyone at the party, if he runs into problems, help will be at least twenty-four hours away. He'll need to be self-sufficient. Making a mental checklist, he remembers the ten essentials from his training, and he checks his provisions one last time before heading out.

Confident he has covered all bases, he heads to the barn to get the Jeep's keys that King keeps on the pegboard in the office. With Stan's increased strength in his left arm and his new lighter leg cast, he is amazed at the ease with which he can navigate along this gravel road that connects the house to the barn. He takes in a deep breath of the country air and throws back his shoulders. It feels wonderful to be independent and to have a purpose as opposed to receiving looks of pity from strangers and family members. Since his accident, those looks are what he has hated the most.

After finding the keys, he approaches the Jeep and grips the steering wheel with his right arm and then with some difficulty, pivots his cast up on the sideboard. From this position he is able to use his upper body strength to lift his rump into the driver's seat. With all of his planning, he failed to calculate the raised height of the Jeep, and immediately it's clear that getting in and out of the vehicle will be his most difficult challenge.

The confidence he was feeling walking down the lane may have been premature, but he is in the driver's seat and this small hiccup is not going to prevent him from moving forward with his plan.

After securing his crutches between the front and back seats, he revs up the engine a few times before throwing the gear shift into drive. Then as if to prove that he's still the speed demon, with a heavy foot on the gas, he turns the steering wheel hard, spinning the tires creating a cloud of dust and stones, and the Jeep makes a three-sixty. Stan is determined not to allow his motorcycle accident to take away his thrill for the ride. He lifts his eyebrows and grins. *I still have what it takes.* The Jeep speeds down the dirt lane.

Earlier he had mapped his route working from the south to the north, exactly in the reverse direction of the cattle drive. This approach would be advantageous as starting in the south would give him practice with the drone and allow him time to tweak any minor quirks unique to this machine before approaching the ravines and steeper slopes in the north.

Stan enjoys the rush of the wind in his face and for the first time since his motorcycle accident he's alive and free. The late morning sun beats down on his head; in his haste he's forgotten his hat. Good thing that sunscreen was one of the essentials and it's in his backpack.

At his first stop, the drone flies beautifully and the controls allow crisp turns, and it accelerates and decelerates smoothly. The video viewed on his screen is clear and when he checks his cellphone, that footage is equally as clear. He's pleased that these photos have a higher resolution than the ones from the older models. He's reminded of the saying that you get what you pay for, as he had spared no expense with this quadcopter. It was three times the price of that first drone he crashed into the side of his condo building just a year before.

Shielding the screen from the sun for better visibility, he scans the image, closely reviewing the two-minute video. If any area is questionable, he will launch the drone a second time in that direction. This method may not be the quickest but is the most efficient.

Out on the trail a little over two hours, Stan has visited less than half the sites marked on his map. The drone has only a five-mile radius so he's careful to drive the Jeep exactly ten miles. Then he stops to scan the area with the drone to be certain that he doesn't leave any area unseen.

He rubs his leg above the cast. Fatigue is setting in as getting in and out of the Jeep is grueling. Maybe he wasn't ready for such an undertaking, as the pain can't be ignored. Being laid up for nearly two months has taken more of a toll on his endurance than he thought. He shakes his head. *Damn this leg.*

Reaching into his chest pocket for the small brown vial he managed to hide in the bookcase of King's office, he takes out a pill and washes it down with a bottle of cold water from the Yeti cooler. He'll push himself and drive to the ridge ahead, just east of the old windmill. That will give time for the pain med to kick in, and he has just enough charge in the drone's battery for one more flight today before calling it quits and being forced to continue the search tomorrow.

Viewing this last feed of video, Stan's eye catches movement near the western slope of the ridge. He resets and views the feed again, concentrating on the last thirty seconds. Yes, something is there and moving. Is it a cow, a horse, or some other animal? He can't identify it as there's a cedar tree blocking his view but he's sure there's something. He checks the battery charge—just fifteen percent, will it be enough? Taking a chance, he launches the drone in that direction, flying as low as possible. He holds his breath as the drone covers the last mile just before the ridge.

Visible on the screen behind the cedar is a saddled horse but without a rider. Stan recognizes the horse; it is Frog. If so, Brett must be out here, but where? Stan steers the drone back and forth around Frog but doesn't see any sign of Brett. The controls show that the drone is headed back. Darn, he needs a few more minutes of battery power. Quickly, he marks Frog's location on the map with a circle.

He's not sure whether it's the excitement of finding Frog or the pain meds taking effect, but the pain from his leg is considerably less intense as he hurries to lift his casted leg up into the driver's seat. He stirs up dust once again as he turns the Jeep and speeds toward the northeast. When near his target, he turns the motor off and listens.

He hears the bellow of a steer followed by a series of grunts as if the animal is in distress. Then he hears a man swearing. With haste Stan climbs out of the Jeep, maneuvers his crutches over the rocky terrain to the cliff and carefully peers over the edge. On the ledge below is a narrow passage, and from the sounds, he knows that there are several cattle there even though he cannot see past the sharp turn. It seems that a steer, in an attempt to back up, had gotten his leg wedged in by a boulder that must have fallen after the rest of the cattle passed, and now it blocks the path, preventing them from retracing their steps.

Stan stares down at Brett, standing by the steer and looking sweaty and dirty with his wet shirt clinging to his chest and a damp, ringed circle on his Stetson. It is obvious that this perfect rodeo stud is frustrated and in much need of help to resolve this predicament. Stan grins as he balances both crutches under the same arm.

"Looks like you have a problem," he yells so that he is heard over the bellowing.

Brett, startled, shields his eyes from the sun with his hand and looks up. "Stan?" he says as if doubting what he sees.

"Last I knew that was my name."

"What are you doing here?"

"Same as you, searching for some stray cattle."

"Really? Well, I'll be damned." Brett breaks into a smile and shakes his head, then his eyes go to Stan's cast.

"I drove the Jeep."

"That makes sense." Brett continues, "This big guy down there managed to get his leg stuck so now all of the others are trapped. There's not enough room for them to pass. We can use the Jeep to move the boulder to the side freeing him, then get the others out. Frog and I can't budge it; it's too heavy, but with the Jeep we should be able to get the job done. Your timing is perfect."

Stan stands taller, pulls his shoulders back and seems to forget about the pain in his leg. "What do you need me to do?"

"Let me get on out of here and I'll give you my thoughts but if you think of something different, speak up. Together we can do this."

After Brett climbs up on the ridge to join him, they discuss some options and decide on a plan. Getting to work, Brett ties the rope that he'd already placed around the rock to the hitch on the Jeep. Then he secures a second rope that he's tied to the steer to the largest tree trunk.

"The halter around the steer's neck will give the animal some support and keep him from rearing back and accidentally falling down the embankment."

Stan appreciates that Brett is explaining each step.

"On my call, give the Jeep some gas. The plan is to first move the boulder just enough to get this guy's leg loose. Then after we get him out of harm's way, we'll work on getting that rock moved to the side so we can clear the path enough to lead the rest of the cattle back out."

Stan nods. "Sounds like a plan."

"Be ready to give the gas when I yell," Brett tells him. "Let's break this big guy loose." He climbs down the ledge and disappears out of sight.

"Okay, ready, give it the gas."

Stan pushes down on the gas pedal.

"More, more, it's not moving."

Stan can't see over the ridge but he hears Brett's commands and puts the pedal to the metal. At first the wheels start to spin on the gravel but then the Jeep moves back ever so slightly. Now he understands why Brett looked frustrated and fatigued; it would have taken the strength of a superhero to move that rock since it must weigh close to a ton.

"It's moving. The rock is moving. Slow...okay, stop."

Meanwhile, Brett directs his rope to the left, guiding the steer forward and away from the rock. "Nice, his leg is out," he yells. "Okay, now try to pull the rock to the right."

Stan repeats the previous process, causing the Jeep's engine to rev but this time turning the steering wheel hard to the right. In a moment he hears Brett yell, "Great, you did it."

Stan stops the Jeep and lets some slack in the rope before putting the Jeep into neutral. He hears nothing so he grabs his crutches and slowly stumbles over to the edge of the ridge. With precision and patience, Brett is guiding the cattle one at a time out of the narrow passage and up on the ridge from an area with a lesser incline.

After all eight cattle are safely on level ground, Stan watches as Brett once again inspects the back leg of the steer that was trapped. "Yep, it's not broken, just bruised. We'll be able to get him back."

Then he makes a cold compress from ice in the cooler and applies it to the steer's leg. "This should make it feel better."

In the meantime, Stan unties the rope from the hitch.

"Great job there, Stan." Brett pats him on the back. "It's good that you came by. I could have never rescued them without your help. How did you find me?"

Stan reaches into the back of the Jeep, pulls out the drone and has just enough battery power remaining to play back the last minute of video footage. Brett's interest in the drone brings out a sense of pride in Stan's voice as he points out its specific capabilities.

As the sun travels into the western sky, Brett checks his new watch. "Damn."

"What's wrong?"

"I need to get moving. The hours are flying by. Gabby will be furious and not to mention embarrassed if I'm not on time tonight. I've got to get those cattle south to join the rest of the herd."

With the excitement of the day, Stan is amazed that he'd forgotten all about the party. "Tell me what I can do to help."

Brett takes off his Stetson and wipes his forehead. "Have you ever herded cattle before?"

"Can't say that I have."

"Well, you want to learn?" Brett flashes his dimple and winks.

"Sure." Stan beams. Did Brett just include him in the task? He knows that he was useful today and even though he must share the success story with the cowboy, he was still a vital part of the team because without the use of the drone and the Jeep, Brett would not have been able to save the cattle. Brett needed his help.

Brett teaches him the basics of cattle herding and finds him a quick study. Stan does a fine job at maneuvering the Jeep behind the herd as Brett rides Frog, moving from side to side in an effort to catch any steer that strays away from the group. It takes them nearly three hours to get the cattle down to the winter pasture but at least the mission is a success.

After getting the cattle with the rest of the herd and introducing Stan to the wranglers, Brett checks his watch and shakes his head.

He turns to Stan. "The boys will take care of Frog. It'll be quicker to ride back to the house in the Jeep with you. The clock is ticking. We've got a party to attend." Brett slaps him on the back and gives a wide smile.

As if the smile is contagious, without effort Stan smiles back. He is beginning to understand how Gabby could be attracted to Brett. He is strong and confident, and knows his way around a ranch. Maybe Brett isn't such a bad guy after all. Would Gabby love a man who wasn't a good person? No, she is smarter than that. Even though Stan still loves Gabby, she has made it clear over these past few months that she doesn't feel the same. When is he going to accept that she is going to build a future with Brett, not him? This is his new family and he really does long to be a part of it. Soon, Brett will also be a member of this family. It is time for Stan to move on.

PART VI

CHAPTER 32

Austin, Texas

U pstairs in the conference room on the second floor of The Gallery, Gabby critiques her appearance in the full mirror. Tonight will be the biggest night of her life. The outward show of wisdom on the face reflecting back must be from the battles she's endured. After coming to terms with her mother's death, along with her failed attempt to showcase her art in New York City, and finally her relationship struggles combined with her grief over the loss of her baby, the woman in the glass appears wiser.

Taking some moments to achieve absolute clarity in an effort to prepare mentally before taking this next step in her life, she evaluates her relationships. First there was Richard. She had repeatedly overlooked his indiscretions in an effort to keep in mind the prize to be first lady in the governor's mansion. Her daddy would have been the proudest Texan, but her unhappiness grew and she was unable to live that lie. After that, she and Brett had a rocky start and took months to repair the damage.

Some would totally consider their engagement a miracle, since that was close to what it took for her to offer him forgiveness. Now, she considers that her forgiveness could have been what prompted him to face his fears and gave him the push to take control of his life. Smiling, she remembers how vulnerable he was as he laid open his soul, much like a tattered book in need of repair. He told her that she made him want to be a better man. He told her of his loneliness—of how she saved his life. Even others have commented how they hardly recognize the once philandering tennis pro. She's surprised at the positive impact she had on his life.

Thinking about Brett and the changes he made, she is reminded of her own life. There was the turmoil she endured when faced with her pregnancy, how she nearly drowned in her tears, thinking she had to choose between her unborn child and the love of her life. When Brett found her in Washington and offered to help raise her baby as his own, was he aware that he saved her? She had lied to him and held the truth from him. This time he was the one who offered forgiveness for her foolish behavior. He made her realize the power of love and showed his commitment to their relationship.

They were two flawed individuals who were brought together under horrific circumstances. After many tears and much forgiveness, their love managed not only to survive but to prosper as well. Her daddy may not have his daughter in the governor's mansion, but she will provide him with a future son-in-law who can carry on the legacy that King has spent his life building. Hopefully, with some luck, Brett and she will also provide King with an heir to carry on that legacy into the next generation.

After analyzing her relationship with Brett and satisfied with the outcome, her thoughts turn to the Equine Assisted Therapy Program. The paperwork forming this nonprofit organization was completed just this week and will receive the profits generated from her art sold this evening. She'll make an announcement tonight and introduce Andrew and Eric, the men whose expertise will get the program running.

Knowing how Stan loved riding prior to his accident, starting this program is her way to apologize for the emotional toll her actions took on his heart. Now it is her time to give back, as this service will help Stan with his rehabilitation as well as helping many other patients. She's glad that her daddy approved of her business venture and dug deep into his pocket to fund it. Maybe some of the other high-profile guests will be inspired by her family's commitment to the therapy program and, after hearing the brief presentation about how the program helps both the physically disabled to regain strength and improve balance and the mentally handicapped to achieve a better quality of life, they too will open their pockets.

Once again she gazes into the mirror and nods in approval of the mature woman. She twirls a blond lock cascading down the side of her face, exposing her golden trinity knot earrings, and continues scanning downward to catch the matching necklace. *Oh, Mother, you would really like him. I wish you could have met.* She draws in her lip determined not to cry.

With both hands she smooths the lace of her elegant pink gown and places her hands on her hips as she turns to view her profile.

The dress fits as if it was made just for her. She straightens her engagement ring and admires its beauty. Making the decision to use this heirloom in place of something modern and trendy was by far the right choice. It sparkles in the bright light and brings a smile to her face. Yes, everything's perfect and tonight will be incredible.

She glances at the clock. *Where is Brett?* He should have been here by now. A knock at the door interrupts her thoughts. Ella bursts through.

"I got here as quickly as I could." Ella stands back after giving Gabby a hug. "Wow, you look totally fabulous."

"As do you, girlfriend. It seems like forever since we saw each other."

Ella places a hand on her stomach. "Look how big I am."

"Ella, it's wonderful...and a girl, lucky you."

"Do you really mean that? I know it must be hard for you, Gabby."

"No, no, it's fine, really." After the words are said, she smiles and interlocks her fingers and brings her hands to her chin. "I love you, silly."

"Thanks, Gab. You're the best."

"Hey, did you see Brett downstairs?" Gabby bites her lip.

"No, but I was in such a hurry to see you I really didn't take notice." Ella sees the worried look on Gabby's face and takes her hands. "Hey, you're not concerned that he'll stand you up? Brett loves you. He wouldn't do that."

"It's just that I wanted us to have a few minutes together before the party starts. We haven't seen each other all week. I stayed here in town to get everything done. I want tonight to be picture perfect."

"Oh, sweetie, it will go off without a hitch. Trust me."

There is another knock on the door and King and Rita enter.

"The guests are starting to arrive," King announces enthusiastically. He looks handsome in his tux, and Gabby can't help but grin for even at his age he's still turning heads.

"Daddy, can I talk with you in private?" She ushers him out the door. "Have you seen Brett?"

"No, kitten, can't say that I have. He must be here. Rusty and Jamie are here and I thought he was leaving the ranch with them. I talked to Rusty earlier, before noon, and he was well on his way."

She wrings her hands. "I think something bad must have happened. No one has seen Brett and it's not like him to ignore my call or text. I've tried now for hours. I know when he drives his convertible with the top down, he can't hear the phone but I'm really starting to get concerned. He should have been here by now." Her voice trembles.

"I'll find him, rope him and drag him here if I have to." He gives her a wink.

She gives a nervous giggle. "Don't you dare. You did that little stunt once already. I can't have him limping around tonight."

"I'll find him. Okay?" He turns her face toward his and kisses her on the cheek. "You look fabulous. He'll be here. Don't worry your pretty little head. Your daddy can and will find him, rest assured." She hangs her head even though she wants to believe him.

He lifts her chin and their eyes meet. "He'll be here. Trust me." She nods.

"Now put a smile on that pretty face and greet your guests. Rita and I came in with Eric and Andrew. Introduce them to my friends.

Talk about the horse program and your art." He gives her a pat on her bottom. "Get going. I'll find Brett."

"Yes, Daddy...and thank you."

Leaving him so he can go on the mission, Gabby returns to the conference room with her head held high.

She opens the door and sticks her head inside. "See you all later." She waves to Rita and Ella and then quickly turns to descend the staircase.

On the main level of the gallery, surrounded by her Hitch series of paintings, she meets her guests without Brett by her side. The three-piece orchestra is playing a lively sonata, and the fragrance of roses fills her nostrils. Minutes later, lifting her eyes up to the second floor where her Zeppelin Bend series is displayed, she finds her daddy waving vigorously from the balcony. He's beaming back at her as if he's glad to get her attention. He nods, gives her the universal thumbs-up sign and then with a raised hand, shows her five outstretched fingers. She nods back. *Wow, that didn't take long.*

She closes her eyes and sighs in relief. If she read his message correctly, King's made contact with her beloved and Brett will be there in five minutes. Her body relaxes but she does make a mental note to mention the desire to kill him for causing her so much worry. It isn't like Brett to cause drama so there must be a good reason.

The sound of a familiar voice brings her back to the receiving line.

"Janet, is that you?" Gabby squeals with delight. "I've missed you. What a pleasant surprise? I didn't think that you could come." She takes the older woman in her arms.

She had met Janet Crystal in Virginia this summer while she was trying to sort out her life. Janet, who owned the Crystal Art Gallery where Gabby first exhibited her Zeppelin Bend series, was her go-to person for motherly advice at that difficult time of her life. And for her support and wisdom, Janet holds a special place in her heart.

"Gabby, I would like you to meet my son, Rob." Janet stands back, allowing her son to shake hands with the guest of honor.

"My mother and Stan have said so many good things about you that I feel I know you already. It truly is a pleasure, Ms. King." He bows his head.

"Thank you." She feels the heat rising in her face, wondering what details Stan has shared with his tall, lean friend with eyes bluer than the sea.

"Terrible accident Stan suffered. I needed to pay him a visit and Mother wanted to see your new series as well as celebrate your engagement, so she closed the shop and we hopped on the first plane to Texas. You should feel honored because I can't remember a time when the gallery wasn't open on scheduled days. Is Stan here? I'm anxious to see him."

Gabby wasn't certain how to answer, not wishing to reveal too much about Stan's condition. Did Janet and Rob know that Stan was in drug rehab? Either way, it wasn't for her to disclose. Thinking fast on her feet, she answered, "He's been getting around on crutches, but the crowd may be too much for him."

She finds herself talking louder as the noise is intensifying. However, it isn't coming from the guests or from the orchestra. Most of the sound is coming from outside the gallery. Janet, Rob and Gabby, as well as the other guests, are drawn to the source of the ruckus.

"Excuse me," she says, politely backing away from her friends while studying the crowd outside on the pavement.

There are reporters with microphones and two camera men. From the large insignia visible on the equipment, they are employed by the local television station. Sure as Richard had warned, he's responsible for the crowd. She notices that he seems totally at ease with all the attention and that Amanda, the tall brunette she met at the ranch, stands holding on to his arm, glowing as if she were the one running for office. He speaks with authority and there is a confidence in his voice. If the election were based on looks, he would easily win as he could win over most of the female voters with a wink or the slightest brush of his hand against their skin. He is dynamic, charismatic, and an eligible bachelor since no ring adorns Amanda's left hand. It's also obvious that Richard is on stage performing for the most influential citizens in the town, and they are a very attentive audience.

Gabby doesn't fault Richard for the noise or the distraction of her guests, drawing their attention away from the art exhibit and the party. Her daddy has paid dearly for Richard's appearance this evening. With the election just weeks away, Richard needs all the visibility he can get to widen the gap in a tight race. To be honest, not being the focus of attention is a welcome relief, and she takes a deep breath and straightens her trinity knot necklace.

Her intuition tells her to glance upward and there on the second-floor balcony stands Brett. He is just watching her as if he doesn't have a care in the world. When their eyes meet, her heart races and she giggles like a schoolgirl. He always has this impact on her: the speeding heart and the quick, shallow breaths. He smiles and his dimple is deep. The urge to run to him overwhelms her and she's drawn to him as a magnet is drawn to the North Pole. The worry he caused with his tardiness is magically forgotten. Without taking her eyes from him, she makes her way through the crowd to the stairs. No one will miss her as their eyes are focused on the candidate for U.S. senator.

As she ascends the staircase, just a few steps from the top, he extends his arm to assist her. His strength and power are intoxicating and her feet seem to have barely touched the ground as she is lifted and embraced. The familiar spicy scent of his cologne permeates her soul. Is she dreaming or is this real? She has longed for this day almost her entire life.

"There you are. I've missed you. It feels good to have you in my arms." He leans down and plants a warm, wet kiss on her lips. "Are you ready?" There is a twinkle in his eyes and he flashes his infamous dimple. "God, you look great."

She stands on tiptoes, brushing her lips close to his ear and whispers, "Yes, and are you sure you want to do this?"

He beams at her, pulls her in again. "Seriously, you're asking me this...now?"

"You're late. I thought you were having second thoughts?"

"Never, my love. I was late because of...well...long story, but Stan helped."

"Helped you to be late? What did he do now?" She backs away and furls her brow. "I warned him. I'll—"

Brett places his finger to her lips to stop her rampage.

"Hey, hey, no, it's not like that. Actually he helped me to get here on time."

"Stan?" Her hands are on her hips.

"Long story like I said, but I can tell you about that later. We've got more pressing matters to attend to now." He places his arm around her waist and swirls her around. "I love you, silly girl."

"I love you too."

"I'm glad because I don't want to live without you."

She twists one of his brown locks around her finger, just staring into his eyes, thinking that she's the luckiest girl on this earth.

CHAPTER 33

Richard and Amanda have entered The Gallery with the camera crew and reporters still underfoot. Some guests give them space while others stand close in hopes of making the local evening news program. Richard stands on the small raised platform just inside the door. He takes a microphone from the violinist and a hush falls over the crowd as he begins his campaign speech, which offers to lower taxes and to put the people's best interest forward. There is nothing unusual or earthshaking. After about fifteen minutes, applause breaks out and the orchestra breaks into a festive tune.

However, the melody is hushed when King appears on the second-floor balcony. Tapping his glass, it is easy for him to get everyone's attention. Well known throughout the state and admired and respected, he's their home-grown oil and cattle baron. His eyes are bright and he radiates positive energy. He stands tall with broad shoulders and the light glistens off his mustaches and white goatee as he waits for complete silence from below. Rita and Stan, along with Will and Ella, stand to King's left, and Gabby and Brett stand arm-in-arm to his right.

Speaking into a cordless microphone, he addresses the crowd.

"Hello, friends! Thank you for coming this evening to celebrate with me and my family. I hope you all enjoyed hearing from Richard Wright, our next senator." The crowd applauds and King waits a few seconds, before tapping on his champagne glass again. "Remember to vote in November.

"Tonight, I am a proud father. Look around you." He motions to all three floors. "This gallery is filled with the amazing artwork of my talented daughter, Gabriella." The crowd claps again. He then looks to Gabby and says, "Honey, your work is beautiful and inspiring, and I understand that one hundred percent of sales goes to the new non-profit Equine Assisted Therapy Program."

There is a rumble throughout the gallery. "That's right. My daughter here is not only beautiful and talented but also desires to help others. There are flyers at the bar. I know all of you will find your way there, so if you have any questions or want to make a donation to this foundation, all of the information is there," he says.

"Also, I want to introduce Andrew Green and Eric Lang. Hey, guys, I know you're out there." King scans the crowd. "Raise your hands and let these fine folks get a look at you." Andrew and Eric walk to the front and center waving their arms in the air.

"These gentlemen run a very successful program in Virginia and they came to Texas to help us start a similar program here. Thank you, boys. So make sure you give them a fine Southern welcome, and if you can dip into your wallet and hand them a Franklin or two, that would be great. It's for a good cause, folks.

"Okay, now to the main announcement before this champagne here in my glass is totally warm, I want to introduce again my lovely daughter and the new state rodeo tie-down champion, Brett Matthews!" Gabby and Brett take a step forward as the crowd applauds once more.

"Kitten, you mean the world to me, and I pray that your sweet mama is looking down on you tonight to see the beautiful woman you have become. You make me proud and happy. You've proven that you're strong and smart." Then he motions to Brett. "Brett, you are an excellent choice for my daughter. I couldn't have picked a better man." His voice cracks. "I welcome you with open arms into the King family. I love you like a son."

Brett sucks in a breath in an attempt to control his emotions. There is a lump in his throat as his dreams of having a family are coming true. There is also some dampness in King's eyes so Rita holds on to his arm for support before he continues.

Regaining his composure, King says, "So all of you here tonight, raise your glasses to help me offer congratulations. It is with pride that I toast to—not an engaged couple pledging their love for one another—but to the newlyweds, Mr. and Mrs. Brett Matthews." He pauses for the buzz around the room to subside.

"Yes, you heard me right. Just a few minutes ago, Brett and Gabby exchanged their vows and became husband and wife. This here gathering is not an engagement party, but we have ourselves a wedding reception."

He raises his glass. "Let's give a toast to Gabby and Brett. May your married life be filled with happiness and everlasting love." The room is quiet for a few seconds as if the guests need to absorb the news flash that King just sprang on them, and then the crowd bursts into thunderous applause.

Gabby and Brett hold up their glasses, toast with the crowd and then follow it with a kiss, as the crowd cheers. The orchestra picks up the festive tune again followed by the doors opening on the main level, and a six-foot-tall wedding cake is rolled into the middle of the room. Cascades of pink roses with gold gems flow from layer to layer of the magnificent multi-tiered cake.

Gabby smiles as her eyes meet Brett's. His dimple is deep and she wants to remember this moment—his expression, the contours of his face, the way his eyes dance and the beautiful curve of his lips. He is handsome, strong and confident, but most of all, he is her husband.

Yes, it was her decision to stop wasting time and to get on with their lives.

It all started a few days earlier when Gabby was painting. While alone at her downtown condo she had called Brett.

"Brett, you awake?"

He rolled over in bed and tried to open his eyes. "What time is it?"

"It's 1:48 a.m. according to my clock."

"Is everything alright?" He sat up in bed and there was a sense of alarm in his voice.

"Brett..."

"What's wrong?" He rubbed his eyes.

"Nothing's wrong. I just needed to ask you something."

"Really, and it couldn't wait until morning?"

"Let's get married."

"We are getting married, right? I asked you and you said yes. I'm confused."

"I want to get married now, before the engagement party." She sucked in a deep breath.

"Really...exactly what do you have in mind?"

"Well, you and me, in front of a minister and we say 'I do.'"

"I thought you wanted a real wedding. You know, the whole big deal: the church, the flowers, the dress, the guests."

"I don't care about all of that. I just want to be married to you." She paused. "I want us to start our life together. Life is too short and this waiting around is ridiculous."

"But we are together."

"I feel like we are in limbo. I know what I want and I want you. Don't you want me?" Her voice quivered.

"Wow..."

"You're hesitating. You don't want to. You're not sure."

"Whoa, Gabby, slow down. Just stop and let me get a word in, okay."

"Okay." She choked back a sob.

"I'm awake now," he said. "Let's start over. Yes, I love you. Yes, I want to marry you. You want to get married tomorrow, hey, I'm all for it."

"Now you're making fun of me."

"No, I'm being serious. I'm not going anywhere and I'm not changing my mind."

"Seriously, you'll marry me...on Friday?"

"Being married to you is want I want. So if my beautiful Gabby wants to get married on Friday, well then, we'll get married on Friday."

"You sure?"

"If that will make you happy, then I'm sure."

"But will it make you happy? I need to hear that you want this as badly as I want it."

"Let's do it. Set it up."

"You mean it?" She chuckled. "There's no turning back once I call Pastor Jim."

"No turning back. Let's get married."

"I love you, Brett Matthews."

"I love you, Gabriella King. Now, go back to sleep."

"I'm so excited I can't sleep. I need to get working on this right away."

"Gabby, I'm excited too but I'm going back to sleep. I'll talk to you in the morning."

Earlier tonight when Richard made his way into the gallery lobby and became the center of attention making his political speech, Gabby and Brett had slipped away to the conference room. With Ella and Will as witnesses, the excited couple stood before Pastor Jim.

Gabby's hands were sweaty as Brett held them to say his vows.

"Gabby, I take you for my wife. You have given purpose to my life. You're my best friend, my reason for waking up each morning and retiring each night. These past few months, your dad and Rita have been the parents I had lost. Once again, I am part of a family.

Princess, you're my everything. Thank you for giving me a second chance. I promise to love you for the rest of my days."

Blinking back tears, Gabby threw her shoulders back. "Brett, your persistence and patience have me in awe. Your ability to overlook and forgive me for all the mistakes I've made makes you a keeper. I promise to share all of my life with you, both the good times and the bad. You make me laugh. You bring me happiness and joy. You bring reason and stability to my life. I'm amazed at the way you love me and the way you say you need me. After all this time, just looking at you still causes my heart to flutter. I promise to love you forever."

After the rings were exchanged, and the minister pronounced them man and wife, Brett picked Gabby off her feet and swung her around in a circle. They'd done it. Now, they were husband and wife.

At the reception, after the cake is cut, the orchestra plays their song, the song that Gabby and Brett first danced to on the back porch of the country club on Valentine's Day. Brett holds her in his arms, thinking this woman in the long pink lace gown is the most beautiful creature alive. He whispers in her ear, "We did it."

"Yes, we did."

"Are you happy, Mrs. Matthews?"

"Very happy. Are you, Mr. Matthews, are you happy?"

"Extremely. Good idea to get married tonight. This evening is the best night of my life. Thank you. I don't know how you pulled this all together. Nothing is ever going to come between us again."

"Nothing will come between us. I'll make sure of that." She gives a slight chuckle.

The party is winding down. More than half a dozen paintings have been sold and nearly twenty grand raised for the EAT program. Brett is at the door speaking with some members from the tennis club when Gabby feels a small tap on her back. It is Stan.

"Hey," he says as he limps closer.

"Hey." Her eyes catch his before she lowers hers to the floor.

He reaches out his right hand and takes her hand. Peering into his face, she sees that his eyes are watery and his efforts to hide his pain are not successful.

"I guess this is where I say congratulations." His voice is a quiet whisper.

"Thank you for your friendship." She manages to hold her eyes to his without looking away. He pulls his hand away.

"You are so special. You know that, right?" She reaches for his hand again.

"Be happy. Promise me you'll be happy. Can you do that?" His eyes move back and forth, scanning her face as if searching for the answer.

"Stan," she chokes, "I never meant to hurt you. I never meant for any—"

He holds his fingers to her lips to signal her to stop talking. "Enough of that, it's all in the past. I'm trying hard to move on. Just promise me you'll be happy."

"Okay, I promise."

"Brett's a lucky man." He drops his crutches on the chair and squeezes both her hands. "May I have this dance?"

She gives a slight smile and points to his leg. "And how is that happening with that cast on your leg?"

"Come on, Gabby, you don't actually believe that this little cast will keep me from dancing with you on your wedding day. You'll be my crutch and we'll just turn around in a small circle like kids do at junior high school dances. You remember, right?" He chuckles.

Without giving her time to respond, he pulls her tight and they turn ever so slowly. Closing her eyes, her thoughts take her to that night in Washington after dinner with Ella and Will, when all four of them went to the club and she and Stan danced. Yes, it's true, at that critical point in her life, she did contemplate a relationship with him, but she didn't love him. Her heart always belonged to Brett.

Seconds later and much to her relief, they are interrupted as Brett taps Stan on the shoulder.

Brett smiles at him. "Thanks for today. Without your help, I might not be married. I don't think Gabby would forgive a man who chose to rescue cattle over arriving on time for his wedding."

Gabby cocks her head at an angle at this seemingly civil exchange between the two rivals.

"Glad I could be of assistance. Gabby's happiness is my number one priority. You're a lucky man to have her as your wife."

"Thanks, Stan. Coming from you that means a lot. So…may I dance with my bride?"

"Absolutely, and congratulations to you both." Stan gives a slight bow as he releases Gabby and stands back to allow Brett to take over.

"Wow, how very civilized. I'm impressed. What happened out there today?" She leans back to study Brett's face.

"He's not so bad, you know." He gives a wink and searches her face for some kind of a reaction.

"I figured that out a while ago. But I'm still confused. What has changed?"

"Game's over, he lost. He knows it and I know it." He pulls her in closer. "I got you and now that we're married, there's just nothing he can do about it."

"Why are you sporting that big, wide grin?" She turns his chin to face her squarely.

"I won and a winner enjoys his prize. What would you say if we got the heck out of this place? I want you all to myself. I've missed you, Mrs. Matthews. We need to consummate this deal."

"I'm a step ahead of you, honey. While you were out on the ranch doing whatever you do out there all day long with Rusty and the other guys, I was here in town arranging everything. I wanted our day and our night to be special. That's why I booked the honeymoon suite at The Driscoll Hotel."

"The honeymoon suite, pretty fancy, darlin' but very appropriate."

"Complete with flowers for me, chocolate chip cookies for you, champagne on ice and beer...and a large tub to soak in while listening to our favorite tunes."

"Sounds perfect. You thought of everything."

"I try. First we need to say a few goodbyes before disappearing, so come along, Mr. Matthews." She takes his hand and drags him across the room.

CHAPTER 34

The following afternoon, all the members of the King family are seated around the table for brunch in the hotel's private dining room. Last evening, the wedding was perfect—the ceremony small and intimate. Now as Gabby looks to each face, her heart swells with gladness. Rita and her daddy are sharing a private conversation, while Ella and Will are busy conversing with Brett and Stan. She's glad the men resolved their differences.

Reaching for her necklace, she moves the trinity knot back and forth on its chain, thinking about how much her family has grown in such a short time. It has more than doubled this year, and the numbers can't be counted just yet, as they anticipate the arrival of her niece. Now Rusty and Jamie come through the door, joining the group, so the circle is complete.

Gabby reaches for Brett's hand and gives it a squeeze. He turns to face her as if to ask, *What?* She smiles and rests her head on his shoulder. He smiles back and puts his arm around her. God knows how much she loves this man. Life is pretty perfect, because it doesn't get any better than this.

Her daddy stands tapping his glass to quiet the noise so he can offer grace. He winks in her direction and she nods her head in approval. After they bow their heads and hold hands, his first words correlate with her thoughts: God is good.

About the Author

DonnaLee Overly graduated from St Petersburg College, Florida in 1983 with an A.S. in Nursing and she worked as a critical care nurse for 20 years before pursuing a degree in studio art from the University of Texas, Austin in 2005. In an effort to mix her art with words, DonnaLee found that the clients responded positively to these expressions of emotions prompting her to continue writing with undeniable passion. This encouraged her to finish her first novel that depicts a female character who expresses her emotions through painting.

Her contemporary fiction novels, THE KNOT SERIES are a trilogy written to give a voice to women's issues that are often hushed.

When she's not painting or playing tennis, she's busy writing.

Visit the author at her website:

www.DonnaLeeOverly.com

The Knot Series

The Knot Series Trilogy unfolds a romantic drama as evil trumps good, using the themes of art, tennis and ranching. The novels untangle struggles and interlock friendships as the main characters achieve emotional healing and self-confidence on their journey to find lasting love.

The Trinity Knot

The Zeppelin Bend (sequel to *The Trinity Knot*)

The Hitch (sequel to *The Zeppelin Bend*)

ACKNOWLEDGEMENTS

It is with mixed feelings that I write the acknowledgements for the final book in THE KNOT SERIES. This journey has been an exciting adventure but sadly it's coming to an end. My hope is that these novels will continue to encourage discussions about emotional topics that are often hushed.

The adventures of Gabby and Brett will remain with me forever. While writing their saga, it was important to have these characters learn from past mistakes, develop patience, and grow emotionally as well as have their love for each other deepen. Even though my novels cover serious situations, filled with raw emotion as a writer who cherishes the reader, I attempted to deliver conclusions that are uplifting and full of hope.

This book could not have been possible without the help of many people to whom I am forever grateful.

Thank you to the experts who shared their knowledge of life on a ranch and rodeo events. You were so patient to answer all of my questions.

Thank you to my wonderful editor, Emily Carmain for making *"The Hitch: knots that bind"* a better book.

Thank you to my publishers, Marie and Mark, at Giro Di Mondo for their support in the continuation of my dream. I have learned so much from you.

Thank you to my husband for his understanding and help to make my dream a reality as well as his continuous love and support.

Thank you to my son for saving my manuscripts, just in case. Mother is extremely grateful! Thank you for believing in me.

Don't miss DonnaLee Overly's next book,

The first book in

The Knot Series II

Coming Summer 2020

True Love Knot
freeing the knot of restraint

Read on for a sneak peek

CHAPTER 1

Rolling on to her back with the hard earth beneath her, Marie was grateful for the thick cloud cover that would soon hide all the stars above. After performing the ritual of the sign of the cross, she allowed her eyes to close in hopes that this nightmare would end, but the heaviness of her breathing and the aching of her body screamed that this wasn't a dream.

Even though the twenty-six-year-old, college graduate fought hard and a fight that would have made her father proud, the wetness that traveled down her cheek cried defeat. For the moment, she had successfully escaped the clutches of her capturers, the men who disrupted her plans to vacation in Cancun with her best friend, Alexis. However, she was ridden with guilt as she couldn't save her friend. Releasing a muffled cry her mind pictured the terror on Alexis' face when after a full day's travel over bumpy roads, the men opened the door to the dark, hot trailer and dragged them through the dirt.

Horror set in as Marie, imagined her best friend's fate-

raped...drugged...killed? No, these men would not kill Alexis as that would make this whole kidnapping senseless.

Taking a deep breath, the pain once again ripped through her left side. Could she have broken a rib as she stumbled in the dark over rocks, crawled through thickets, and waded through streams and creek beds? She ran her tongue over her dry, cracked lips and tasted blood. The bleeding didn't matter, nothing mattered. She had exhausted all of her strength and her wits to escape, knowing that if they caught her, they would punish her for disobeying. However, she was determined not to be a pawn in the game of drug smuggling and human trafficking.

Now there was no more running, not one more step. Marie could not crawl or claw her way another inch. She was done. Her wet clothes were cold as they clung to her body and she shivered. Sometime during her prayer for both herself and Alexis, the darkness won the battle.